Carrington Legacy

Also by T. C. Florer

Rural Iowa Ruins

Against the Current

Reflections Along the White Pole Road

One More Turn on the Two Lane

Carrington Series

Unfinished Vow

Dawn's Renaissance

Carrington Legacy

And in the fall of 2015

Full Circle

The legacy of Chet and Dawn carries on in this volume. We first met them, as readers, in the novel *Unfinished Vow*, followed by *Dawn's Renaissance*. We were with them as they experienced full lives, rich in love, hope, happiness, and loss.

You, as readers, continued to inquire. What happened next? I was blessed to be included, almost like a family member. It was paramount to Dawn that the family story should be told, going forward, in hopes of touching at least one life.

And it has touched mine.

Timothy C. Florer

Carrington Legacy

By T.C. Florer

Copyright© 2015 By Timothy C. Florer

Published by Timothy C. Florer
Diana Willits, Editor and Project Director
Designed and edited by Leng Vong Reiff, Akili Design & Marketing Services, Inc.
Barb Drustrup, Literary Advisor
Cover art by Leslie Leavenworth
First edition March 2015
ISBN: 9780692406397

This book is a work of fiction. Names, characters, places, and incidents are either a product of the author's imagination, or are used coincidentally. Any resemblance to actual persons living or dead, events, or locations, is entirely coincidental.

Proudly printed in the U.S.A.

All rights reserved. No part of this book may be reproduced, or transmitted in any form by any means, electronic, mechanical, photocopying, recording, or otherwise, without prior permission of the publisher.

To Ann Donohoe, who listened to me explain that I had a story in my mind for years, and she replied, "You need to write it down to get it out of your head." Her astute wisdom has led to four novels, and I feel blessed for knowing her.

To Polly Clark, whose gentle use of her editor's red pen, encouraged me to peel back more of my personal layers, exposing deeper insight and emotion.

To Leng Vong Reiff, whose elegant sophistication of design allowed my thoughts and words to become illuminated.

And to Diana Willits, whose skills and knowledge of the publishing arena guided four of my creations to the finish, her confidence in me never wavering.

Working with all of you has made me a better person.

Thank you!

Chapter 1

Ten years have passed in a blink of an eye. Dawn mentioned to Wren, Meadow, and Lark that the older she had become, time flew by much too fast, as if she were on a bobsled, streaking down hill, faster and faster. She always cautioned them, "Don't be in a rush to grow up. It will be on you soon enough, and you can't recapture your youth."

They were here today, Wren, a stunning beauty with red hair, age 24, Meadow, tall and lean, her strawberry blonde hair catching the sun's rays, age 23, and Lark, a compact blonde, who, at age 22, still possessed the stride and demure of an athlete.

They all gathered with Dawn to take in the ambiance that was before them. On a slight rise stood a pergola, its sensual curved rafters covered in pink, white, and red climbing roses. The center of the structure framed the eye pleasing view that spread out before them. Row after row of heavy laden grape vines, La Crescent, Brianne, and Marquette, all in equal numbers, created a contrast with the roses that would surely excite a Renaissance painter. And the combined scents were intoxicating! Harvest was scheduled to begin in ten days, right after the wedding.

Each of the four females held, in their hands, a copy of the vows that would be spoken by the bride. They had all contributed, yet only one had the final say, and they all had a pact that the groom would not know the words until she had spoken them.

The final draft had been printed by hand on a luxurious sheet of velum stationary that had been dyed with just a hint of a soft pink hue. She had planned to frame it after the ceremony and hang it above their king sized bed.

Before they left to check on the final arrangements, she asked, "Would you all please stay for another minute and listen while I read this out loud one more time? "They all smiled and nodded yes. She took her place in the pergola, captured a deep breath to calm her inner self, and began to read the words she had wanted to say for such a long time.

My Darling,

This is the moment I have waited for my entire life. I believe every little girl dreams of finding her prince, and with God's blessing, I have found you.

My love for you started as a curiosity, a wonderment, and then it slowly evolved. I hid it from you, wanting to make sure it was from my heart and soul, not just a fantasy.

When I knew you felt it, too, our love grew together, building layer on layer of trust, respect, kindness, and the art of becoming one.

We took our time, with you always saying, "You must be happy and content with yourself before we head towards a night of continuous tomorrows. "I love your patience. You let me grow as a person, unencumbered by a set of society's guidelines. I found myself, and today, I give all of my soul, love, and body to you, in trust that you will dedicate the same to me.

With this ring, I thee wed.

Ten years earlier

The first annual Chester T. Carrington Memorial Writer's Workshop had just finished, and the reviews, including one in the *Iowa State Daily*, gave Dawn a glow of pride knowing Chet would have been happy with the outcome. The twenty participants came away with a set of fresh ideas, gleaned not only from the class, but also the one-on-one conversations that usually went late into the night.

All of the writers were required to critique the job that Chris Cody, their instructor, had done. He had personally told them, "I brought my thick skin. I am prepared for brutal honesty."

After the students left to travel back to their homes, Dawn and Chris went to the Memorial Union for coffee, and to review the conference. Chris asked Dawn to read the critiques out loud to him, and she began, "Such a serious person for his age." "I am thirty years his senior, but he brought up points I had never thought of." "It is rare for any person to bring honest emotion to a discussion, but he surely did." "Such a grasp of feelings and emotions. It was either God given, or inherited, or both!"

Dawn's favorite was from a middle-aged female, "I could listen to his voice for hours, his manners were impeccable, and his looks were really easy on the eyes!" Dawn chuckled as she reached across the table to pat Chris' hand, and said, "I would say you inherited a lot of your father's qualities." She then asked him what he thought of the experience.

"Dawn, I must first thank you for the opportunity to teach the first event to honor my Dad. That word, Dad, is still new to me, but I am loving that word more each time I say it. What a thrill to teach in the same room as he did, to sit on the same stool as he sat, and to admire the new portrait that you commissioned Leslie Levenworth to paint of him. It will always be displayed here in the Chester Carrington Memorial Hall.

The past few days, I have walked in his shadow, from the theatre where he watched *Love Story* with Michelle, to the fourth step by the Union where they sat, and past the President's House, where he and you had your first dinner.

His presence is all encompassing, not only in this place, but in the hearts and minds of all the people he touched through his writings. To have my name associated with his is the greatest compliment I will ever receive. Dawn, again, thank you!"

Dawn replied after wiping the tears from her cheeks, "I know he is up there, smiling, as you and I sit here and talk about him.

You mentioned that you could stay here a little longer. I would suggest that you drive to the cabin on Black Duck, and stay there for a few days. Chris, your father spent more than thirty years of his life there, being refreshed and rejuvenated by the sights and sounds, and that is where his body rests, next to Michelle. If you wish, I will contact the Hansons and have them prepare for your arrival."

Chris reached across the table, and gently laid his hand on Dawn's, "I would so much appreciate that, thank you! How soon may I go?" Dawn replied, "Remember, tomorrow, Sadie and her three granddaughters are coming by for supper. You should be able to leave the following morning for the cabin. I will call the Hansons tonight. Now, come on, I will treat you at your Dad's favorite restaurant!"

They arrived at Hickory Park, received their number, were finally seated, and dove into the sampler plates, followed by Turtle sundaes.

Chapter 3

Dawn arose with the sunrise, and noticed Chris' rental car was already parked next to the office. After the coffee was brewed, she delivered a cup to Chris, who smiled that Carrington smile, and told her he couldn't sleep, and was reading, for the third time, Chet's novel in the red binder. He politely offered Dawn an opportunity to discuss the book, but she declined, again stating it was for his eyes only. She invited him to walk with her to the grove, so they could relish the morning. He agreed, and she grabbed a thermos and cup for herself, and they leisurely walked, taking in all the scents that the morning dew had refreshed. When they arrived, she gestured to Chris to take Chet's chair. When he settled in, he felt a warm, enveloping breeze surround him, and Dawn noticed the quizzical look on his face. She let out a laugh and said, "Yes, there have been unexplained things happening here for years. I believe we are not alone. My advice, accept it all without explanation. Your father would talk about hearing the call, and accepting it. I know he would advise you to open your soul to all possibilities." Chris closed his eyes, and a few moments later, he whispered to Dawn, "This is where he was when he died, in this chair. But I also sense that someone or something was here, also." Dawn softly answered, "I believe that Michelle helped guide him to his next step to eternal life."

They sat quietly and listened to the symphony that was coming from the marriage of the wind and the pine boughs, and were comfortable knowing that words were not required.

Chapter 4

Their stay in the grove lasted past noon, when they finally headed towards the house. Dawn had a list of things that had to be done in preparation for dinner that night. Chris pitched in, dusting and vacuuming, while Dawn readied the kitchen and bath. While they worked, Dawn filled Chris in on the details of Sadie and her granddaughters. She mentioned how the girls were her first students in the writing program that Chet had suggested, how they had really helped her deal with her grief, and that their book, *The Petersen Sculptures Midnight Escape*, had risen to the top of children's books list, thanks to thousands of sales to ISU alumni for their children and grandchildren.

Chris asked Dawn to let him see a copy of it, so he would be able to converse with the girls on a common subject. She handed him a copy, and thought, "What a kind person he is, wanting someone else to feel comfortable. Just another inherited trait!"

Sadie and the girls arrived, and Dawn introduced Chris to them. Lark said, "I Googled you. You are pretty famous!" Meadow mentioned she liked his poetry, especially the award winning *Missed*, and Wren became flushed when she shook hands with Chris. He complimented all of them on their book, then said he needed to tend to the barbecue. After he went outside, Sadie remarked how much he looked like Chet in the painting on the living room wall. Lark thought he looked "hot" for an old guy, and Meadow agreed. With her face still flushed, Wren said, "I should take these steaks outside and supervise him. I am sure he has never cooked Iowa beef." Dawn laughed while she handed the plate of steaks to Wren, and reminded her that all the females liked medium rare.

While the steaks were cooking, Chris and Wren had a conversation of what the girls next book would be about, what Wren's classes next fall in high school would be, farming, and vineyards. Chris mentioned that he and his mother were part owners of a vineyard in Oregon, and that he had noticed a lot of them in Iowa as he had driven on the two-lane roads. Wren added, "I think that your father served an ice wine to Dawn on the night they became engaged. It came from a winery just north of Ames. Someday you should visit there."

By then the steaks were ready, and a wonderful dinner was enjoyed by all. Afterwards, Dawn and Sadie commented that the best part was the conversations that seemed to fly around the table, and that the three girls could hold their own.

After the Russell family said their goodbyes, Dawn finally reached the Hansons by phone, and they were more than happy to ready the cabin for Chris' visit the following afternoon.

Over coffee, Dawn showed Chris the location of the cabin on the map. She also gave him the name of the grocery store and bakery in Ash Lake where he could stop and pick-up provisions. Chris prepared to return to the hotel, telling Dawn he wanted to get an early start in the morning. Dawn replied, "I will give you some free advice. While you are there, open your soul completely. You might be surprised by what you may receive. Drive safe." They hugged, and she watched him drive down the road.

When she went back inside, the phone was ringing. She answered. It was Brent Makenzie.

"It is so good to hear your voice," said Dawn. "I wanted to thank you again for the dozen yellow roses you sent me before the workshop started, and the card, *With Anticipation*, expresses my feelings, also. So, are we still on for our date tomorrow?" After a pause, Brent replied, "That's why I was calling. I have an idea I wanted to visit with you about. I propose that you come up to my place in Lanesboro. With three bedrooms and two baths, there will be plenty of room, we will be just a few minutes walk from the Root River, and you would be the first woman to cross my threshold since I moved in. Dawn, you have said you admired my honesty, and I would be more comfortable here with you than at your home. Your past life is still there, and an inner voice inside me doesn't want to compete with that, yet. Can you understand?"

After a long pause, Dawn replied, "Thank you for your honesty, and I think it is healthy that we can have this discussion. I would relish the thought of you and I just being together, enjoying each other's company, with no pressure. I understand you not wanting to be in the shadow of the past, and I, too, would like to start our relationship on fresh ground. Neither one of us knows how this will end up, but we owe it to ourselves to have an unencumbered chance. So, when should I arrive, and what should I bring?"

With a sigh of relief, Brent answered, "Tomorrow would be great. I suggest both an inside and an outside wardrobe. I will e-mail directions, and you should count on a three-hour drive. Please call me when you are a half-hour away, and I will have lunch ready. "With a smile on her face, Dawn replied, "I look forward to being with you, Brent!"

Chapter 6

The next morning as Dawn was leaving home to drive to Lanesboro, Chris was already on the road making his journey to the cabin. He headed up I-35 into northern Iowa, passing mile after mile of corn and bean fields. He stopped north of the Twin Cities at Forest Lake, for gas and a burger and fries. Following the map, he exited of I-35, just south of Duluth, onto Highway 33 that took him through the town of Cloquet. He stopped and took a half hour to study the only Frank Lloyd Wright service station in America, built on the banks that overlooked the river.

From there he continued north and picked up Highway 53, making note of how the terrain now consisted of granite rocks and pine trees.

He finally pulled into Ash Lake, and stopped at the grocery store to buy supplies to make his traditional Carrington dinner, which included: coffee, bread, lunch meat, cheese, milk, cereal, steaks, potatoes, butter, and the fixings for salad. Dawn had assured him there would be a great selection of wine inside the cabin.

After loading the groceries into his car, he continued on towards the cabin, arriving within ten minutes. Harry Hanson was waiting for Chris in the driveway. He introduced himself, and said, "Chris, I am here to show you how everything works in the cabin." Harry helped him inside with the groceries and his suitcase, and gave him the tour, showed him the thermostat, and remarked that the linens on the bed were fresh, along with the towels in the bath. He then asked Chris to follow him down to the boathouse. As Harry lifted the door, Chris caught his breath as he caught the first glimpse of his father's boat, a 1938 Chris Craft Barrel Back. It seemed that it had just come off the showroom floor, absolutely perfect in every way. Chris got a lump in his throat when he read the name painted in gold on the transom, *Author*.

Harry jumped into the cockpit and showed Chris the controls while he started the engine. The sound was like a classic Harley Davidson; a deep and powerful rumble that exuded raw power.

After shutting down the engine, Harry showed him where the life jackets were stowed, and a map of the lake. He told Chris, "Every red ink dot on this map is a place where Chet caught walleye. He always said that this map was as important as his best selling books, and he never shared it with anyone. Dawn instructed me to give it to you as a welcoming gift. All of his fishing tackle is over in the cabinet.

Now I will leave you to some peace and quiet. Here is my card, call if you need anything." Harry then pointed his finger towards the knoll above the cabin and said, in a reverent tone, "The other place you came to see is up there. He was one helluva man's man." With those final words, Harry left, and Chris began to soak in all the Chet Carrington ambiance.

He slowly walked back up to the cabin, and paused on the deck that offered a view of the lake. The surface was as still as a mirror, perfect for skipping flat stones. Chris cautioned himself to take a deep breath, throw off all his tension and anxiety, so his soul could soak in all that would come before him in this special place.

As he went inside, his eyes were drawn to the beautiful baby grand Steinway, its rich patina illuminated by the light from two picture windows. Dawn had mentioned to him that this was the first piano she played, and it had helped solace her in times of loss and pain. He gently lifted the cover, and caressed the ivory keys. A memory from his past came forward, and he could see himself at his 6th grade music recital. All of the students at his private school academy had to learn to play at least one instrument, and his mother, Katherine, had chosen the piano for him. He laughed out loud as he pictured himself at piano lessons, constantly peeking at the wall clock, counting down the minutes until the torture was over. The piece he played at that recital was *Over the Rainbow*. He thought, "Why not!" He pulled out the bench, sat down, and closed his eyes as he gently laid his fingers on the keys. As he played the first note, the rest of the composition seemed to flow from his fingertips, and he played it, flawlessly. A single tear formed in each of his eyes as he wondered, "Dad, did you hear that?"

He slowly stood up, closed the cover, and replaced the bench. He wandered into the kitchen, found the coffee maker, filled it, and it began to brew. He noticed that even the smell of fresh brewed coffee seemed more pure here.

He took his cup and walked to the front door, opened it, and stood at the threshold. His eyes followed the contour of the land as it rose to the top of the knoll. He took a step, and hesitated. He decided to take that walk after supper, just before sunset. Going back inside, Chris freshened his coffee, and went out on the deck. He pulled a chair close to the railing so he could rest his feet, and laid his head against the back of the chair. The warm sun on his face caused him to close his eyes, and sleep came over him.

And he dreamed.

He must have been age three or four, dressed in his school uniform. A white, short sleeve dress shirt, red tie, tan slacks, and brown penny loafers. A large landscaped park was next to the main school building. Fog lay heavy in the morning, and the brick pathways that wound through the grass seemed to disappear. He saw himself, running, his arms reaching forward, calling out, "Wait for me, I can't see!" No answer. He continued running, while shouting, "Please!" Still no answer. His next step slipped on a wet brick, and he went down, landing on both knees, ripping his slacks, and skinning the palms of his hands.

As he stood up, he looked at his scraped hands, his lower lip quivering, when a figure appeared out of the fog. It seemed human, but had no facial features. It gently wrapped him up in an enveloping embrace, and said, in a low, gentle voice, "I am here for you, it will be all right. You are safe." A warm feeling spread through his small body as he thought, *someone does care!*

The mournful call of a loon brought Chris back to reality. The large male was swimming towards the boathouse, then dove underwater, surfacing on the other side of the dock. Chris thought of a passage from his father's book in the red binder, about how the loons had actually given him comfort when he was at a low, desperate time in his life. By just watching and listening, Chris understood.

He decided to have dinner before taking that emotional walk to the knoll. After grilling a filet mignon, he made a salad, and selected a premium Merlot from the wine cabinet. He moved back to the deck to dine, wanting his senses to be washed by all the beauty before him. While he took his first bite, he imagined that Chet sat at this exact same spot, eating his dinner, countless times. Chris was glad that he had heeded Dawn's advice.

After finishing dinner, Chris poured one more cup of coffee, and returned to the deck. He noticed that the moon was just beginning to rise on the horizon, and that was his clue to begin his walk up the knoll. He went inside, put his cup in the kitchen sink, grabbed a light fleece jacket, and walked out the front door. He calmed himself with a few deep breaths, and began his trek up the hill.

      The closer he got, the slower he walked. When he finally arrived, he first noticed the contrasts of the sky. The sun was setting on his left, and the moon glow was coming from his right. The combination of light illuminated the stark white tombstone with the black lettering. He stood above it, tears beginning to wash his face, as he read:

Chester T. Carrington
1952-2012

Husband to Michelle Bastien
Then
Husband to Dawn Wilson

He touched people with words

      As he stepped around the backside of the stone, he noticed fresh etchings in black, set in the stone:

Father of
Christopher Cody
Born to Katherine Cody
September 20th, 1988

      Chris fell to his knees, holding on to the top of the stone with his hands. His heart seemed to be on the verge of exploding as a river of tears fell from his cheeks. There, for all to see, was the validation he had craved all his young life, to be announced by a father that he was a son.

As all of his emotions were rising in his soul, Chris heard the voice from his dreams, but it was there, at that exact moment in time, clear and succinct, "I am here for you, son. It will be all right."

A warmth of fulfillment encompassed Chris, and he raised his face to the sky, and whispered, "Thank you."

Chapter 7

The same moon that shone on Chris was illuminating the living room of Brent Makenzie, just outside Lanesboro. Brent and Dawn were sitting across from each other in comfortable wing chairs, their legs resting on ottomans.

The air was filled with a relaxed atmosphere as they reviewed all the things they did that day. Dawn had arrived at noon, and after a light lunch, they drove into town and rented bicycles. As they rode on the Root River State Trail, Dawn thought of how great an idea it was, "New territory, no baggage or responsibilities, just two adults enjoying each other's company." The trail was a thing of beauty, surrounded by limestone bluffs, hardwood forests, and the river.

They had decided to have an early dinner, so after turning in their bicycles, they went to the Riverside on the Root restaurant. Being early enabled them to have a table at the water's edge. Brent was amazed at how their conversations just seemed to flow. It seemed they had been life-long friends with no need to impress or embellish the truth.

Before they drove back to Brent's, they stopped at the local bakery and purchased two slices of strawberry covered cheesecake. He assured Dawn they were low calorie, and he had a perfect wine to pair it with. She raised her eyebrows and said, "Really? Low calorie? Cheesecake?" They laughed about her comment as they pulled into the driveway. They went inside to the kitchen and Dawn placed the cheesecake in the refrigerator.

As she turned around, Brent gently took her hand, and looked deep into her eyes. He whispered, "I am so thankful that you are here. It's important for me to tell you, I have no expectations for this weekend. I don't want you to feel any pressure, I sincerely enjoy the simple pleasure of your company."

Dawn stepped into him and kissed him full on the lips, then whispered breathlessly, "Thank you for those words. I believe you mentioned a great wine, I think it's time!" Brent smiled and pulled two crystal wine glasses from their holder, and poured. They walked into the living room and sat in the chairs.

The conversation turned to Brent's photography. He told Dawn that he recently viewed his entire body of work, and had selected twenty-five images. He continued, "These represent the best images from all the countless shoots I have been on for the past twenty-some years. I plan to have them framed, and find a venue to hold the Brent Makenzie retrospect. I would like to share them with you, on the condition that you give an honest, even brutal, opinion." Dawn happily agreed, and Brent laid the collection on the dining table. Together, they slowly viewed each one. Brent informed Dawn why each was taken, the weather conditions at the time of composition, and what he felt inside after he had tripped the shutter. The insights that he revealed opened a nuance that Dawn had yet to see, and it pleased her that he would share those intimate details with her. She thought, "This is what it should be, getting to know how someone feels about a subject, the emotions behind decisions made, the pride of self accomplishment."

When they finished critiquing the last image, Dawn noticed that it was 11:00PM, and stifled a yawn. Brent noticed, and suggested they eat their cheesecake. Dawn agreed, and they picked up the images from the table, Brent returned them to the cabinet, and Dawn retrieved the dessert from the kitchen. They slowly ate, enjoying the luxury of the taste, while they both felt surrounded by a serene feeling of comfort and assuredness, that this is where they should be, together, in this moment in time.

Brent cleared the table, and slowly approached Dawn. He embraced her tenderly, gently kissed her lips, and quietly said, "It has been a long day, yet one of the best in my life. Since you crossed my threshold, it has felt like Christmas morning. Thank you! Let's get some sleep, and make new memories tomorrow."

With that said, they retired to separate bedrooms to dream of the possibilities.

The following morning, the sun had cut through the fog, giving way to a cloudless sky over Black Duck Lake. Chris had slept peacefully, feeling his universe was more in alignment than ever before. His first thought that morning was about a puzzle. When he was young, his mother taught him to find all the edge pieces first, then fill in towards the middle. He realized that the experience he had the previous evening filled a large part of his life's puzzle, and he looked forward to the quest of finding even more pieces.

After breakfast, he called Harry to ask where he needed to go to get a fishing license and minnows. He gave Chris the name and directions to the bait shop, and also said, "Here is a tip. Buy one dozen eight ounce pink jigs. Tip them with medium-sized minnows, and you will have your limit by noon. If it were me, I would try just below the falls first. You will find it marked on your Dad's map. Good luck!"

After Harry hung up, Chris smiled, he loved that word, "Dad!" He found the bait shop, purchased everything he needed, then stopped at the bakery to buy one-dozen chocolate chip cookies. He thought they would hit the spot, mid-morning, with some coffee from a steaming thermos.

He arrived back at the cabin, and changed clothes. Out of the corner of his eye he noticed the closet door was slightly open, and being curious, Chris looked inside. Before him were ten flannel shirts, all in a large checkered pattern, and each one had a well-worn left sleeve. He took a red one off the hanger, and slipped it on. Immediately, he noticed a familiar scent, the same one he gave off after a workout. A lump formed in his throat as he thought that he smelled like his father, just one more connection, another piece of the puzzle. Out loud, he proclaimed, "Dad, if it's okay, I am making this my fishing shirt!"

He closed the closet door, and made his way to the boathouse. He opened the door, and caught his breath, again. The beauty and design of *Author* was far superior to any craft built today. Chris put on his father's life jacket, and grabbed two spinning reel and rod sets, a tackle box, net, and his minnow bucket. He studied the map, and started the engine. After it warmed up, he cast off the mooring ropes and backed out of the slip.

Using his compass and map, he headed north in the main channel. He remembered the rhyme he learned at the Columbia River Yacht Club where he took sailing lessons as a teenager, "Left of the red, right of the green, when you are going upstream." He found the first buoy marker, and proceeded towards the falls.

As he drove, he became very emotional, thinking, "I am touching the steering wheel that Dad had touched, the gear shift, ignition key, all have his DNA, and now they have mine. These are some of the markers I mentioned in my poem, *Missed*. More pieces added to the puzzle!"

He finally pulled into the bay that captured the falls. He positioned the boat where the red dot was on the map, shut off the engine, and placed a minnow on the jig. He cast toward the falls, and before he could feel the lake bottom, a hungry walleye was running off with his bait. Chris set the hook, and wound in the fish to the boat, netting the three-pound beauty. After sliding it on a stringer, he looked to the sky and said out loud, "Dad, thank you, this will be supper tonight!"

He set his rod aside, and poured a cup of coffee from the thermos, and began to eat a few cookies. He opened up his soul, as Dawn had suggested, and with sight and breath, he took in all the ambiance that lay before him, the sound of water falling, the wind gently moving the birch leaves, the small waves kissing the bow of *Author*. He wondered how many times Chet had been in this same spot, seeing what Chris saw now, feeling this almost religious experience, the sharing of two generations aligned in a single moment.

He spent the rest of the morning catching and releasing more walleye, until a growl in his stomach suggested it was time for lunch. He headed back to the cabin, thinking , "It doesn't get any better than this!" as he took in the scenery. When he caught site of the cabin, he also noticed signs posted on the properties that bordered Chet's land. He made a mental note to investigate them after lunch.

He put *Author* inside the boat house and stowed all the gear exactly as he had found it. He found a fish cleaning board and fillet knife in the locker, and took his walleye dock side to clean it. He rinsed the two fillets in the cool lake water, along with the knife and board, leaving them on the dock to dry.

Entering the cabin, he laid the fillets on paper towels, and began to prep for lunch. Potatoes were peeled and sliced razor thin, a lettuce salad was made, and the cast iron skillets became hot, the oil just on the verge of smoking. As the potato slices began to cook to a golden brown crisp, he laid the coated fillets gently in the hot pan, carefully turning them after three minutes. He plated the fillets and chips, set them on the table with his salad, and poured a glass of wine. As he took his first sip, he thought, "I can imagine sitting here with you, Dad, eating this exact meal, while we talked about the one that got away. I can feel your presence here, and I am content."

      He slowly ate, savoring each bite, while listening to the waves splash on the dock. From a distance he could hear loon calling for its mate. After finishing lunch and cleaning up, Chris went back to the dock to put the now dry board and knife back in the boat house. He then headed up to the knoll, and noticed a young couple just leaving the grave site. As they pulled away, he saw Harry walking toward him. Chris waited, they shook hands, and before Harry could ask, Chris said, "Best day of fishing I ever had!" Harry nodded, and Chris continued, "Do you know that couple that just left the grave site?" Harry responded, "No, I sure don't, but it has been this way ever since your dad was buried. It first started out with just one or two people stopping a week, and the flow has increased since then. Sometimes they take a pencil and trace his name on a piece of paper, some of them have left copies of his books, and some leave bouquets of flowers. I take the books to the Ash Lake Library and donate them, and I leave the flowers until they wilt, then dispose of them." Harry paused, and continued, "Now Chris, there is one other thing. It started the month after Chet passed, and has continued. On the first day of each month, a dozen red roses are sent to the grave from the florist at Ash Lake. The card always says the same thing, "Thank you for the gift." I was curious after about three months, so I asked Nell, the florist, what the deal was. She had received a phone call after the burial, with instructions that each month, those roses and card were to be delivered, and she received a check for a five year supply in the mail. Nell said the check cleared, so she is going to deliver her part of the deal. Any idea who it is?"

      Chris paused, then replied, "Evidentially, my father touched the life of someone, the gift could be anything from money to an emotion or idea that they read in one of his books. It is just one of those things in life that needs no explanation, just acceptance. Harry, thank you again for keeping this spot pristine. Now, can you tell me about the properties that are for sale on each side of Chet's?"

Harry suggested that they walk the properties, so Chris looked at the gravestones, then followed Harry down the hill while he began to fill Chris in on the details.

"The properties are the same size, they both have 2,000 feet of shoreline. The north one was never developed, it is still virgin land. The one to the south has a dilapidated cabin, roof falling in, and brush choking the yard. The north property had been tied up in litigation for years, grandchildren fighting for dollars. The south one is owned by an elderly widower from Duluth who is now in a nursing home. Somehow, the man's only nephew now has power of attorney, and was trying to cash in. Each property was priced the same, $250,000, and the realtor in Ash Lake had the listings for the past two years."

Harry reached into his pocket, retrieved his wallet, and took out a business card. He handed it to Chris, saying, "That's the realtor, nice guy, been here as long as I have. He could never work up the courage to talk to Chet. Guess he never will." Harry put his hands in his pant pockets and shook his head, whispering, "I still miss him."

Chris patted Harry on his shoulder, and replied, "I will be leaving in the morning. I will take *Author* out one more time before I go. Thank you for all your help, and I promise you will see me again, soon." Chris began to walk to the cabin when he heard Harry say, "He would be damn proud of you, that I know." Chris waved thank you to him as his eyes began to fill with tears, hoping Harry was speaking the truth.

Chapter 9

That same afternoon, in Lanesboro, Dawn and Brent had just finished lunch, and had decided to go into town to rent the bikes again. They headed out in the opposite direction from their trip the day before, and were again, impressed by what they saw. The limestone bluffs along the river were tall enough to keep the trail in shade most of the day, and they heard the constant melody the water sang as it moved over and around rocks that were in the path of the flow.

On the high ground, they passed through small apple orchards and farms that had begun to cater to the "Eat Local" crowd. There were acres of lettuce, onions, tomatoes, green beans, and carrots. Dawn and Brent both agreed that on the way back, they would purchase produce to go along with the steaks that Brent had laid out for supper.

When they reached the turn-around point, they sat in the shade and drank their water. Brent looked into Dawn's eyes, and asked, "Would you please tell me more about the girls, I really enjoyed their book that you sent me to read." Dawn smiled, and began, "You need, no, I want you to know how important they are to me. They came into my life at a time when the future looked bleak, I had really no desire to move forward. Working with them instilled hope in my heart, and I re-discovered that innocence and honesty comes with youth. It is only as we mature that we build up that wall around our soul for protection. Being with them has helped heal my heart, and I have told all three of them that I got much more out of the arrangement than they did.

Now, they are being mentors to the next group of students that are enrolled in our workshop. Brent, imagine being fifteen, and learning from a girl your own age who has published a book. It really gets the new students' attention.

Now, enough about them. If we don't get back on our bikes soon, I will be too stiff to pedal!" With a hearty laugh from Brent, they began the journey back. They stopped at a roadside produce stand

and purchased lettuce, tomatoes, and strawberries that were bursting with ripeness. When they arrived in town, they turned in their bikes and stopped at the store next door to buy a quart of dairy fresh heavy cream.

At Brent's house, Dawn excused herself to shower, and Brent started the grill. He went inside to the kitchen to prepare the salads, and halfway through, Dawn emerged, dressed in a yellow sundress that was cut in a way that caught Brent's attention. His eyes moved over her, and she shyly asked, "Do you like what you see?" His reply, "Stunning!" "Breathtaking." He took her right hand and lightly kissed it, and said, "If I take a quick shower, will you finish the salads?" She nodded yes, and he took one long look at her, and then showered. Minutes later, he emerged, dressed in tan shorts and a pink polo shirt. Dawn smiled and said, "I approve, and the salads are done."

Brent said he would throw on the steaks, and Dawn picked a nice Merlot to have with dinner. She poured two glasses full, then moved to the patio to watch him, to imagine what he would be like. Those thoughts made her flush, and he noticed her gazing at him, and smiled. He was having thoughts of his own.

The steaks were perfect, as was the conversation. Brent proved that he was still a world-class listener. He wanted to know all about Chris and the workshop, and Dawn filled him in on the details. She finished by explaining to Brent that Chris was at the cabin on Black Duck, and she was looking forward to visiting with him about the feelings he experienced while walking in his father's footsteps.

After dinner, Brent poured each of them another glass of wine, and they sat on the deck, watching the sunset begin to paint the late evening sky, with the Root River reflecting a mirror image of the sky's beauty. They sat, holding hands, not speaking out loud, but communicating with their eyes and gentle touches, touches that aroused their inner senses.

Brent stood and suggested they go inside. He turned on the CD player and lit two candles on the dining table. He took Dawn in his arms and they began to dance to the melodies of Barry Manilow, the same music they had danced to in Burlington, over two decades ago. Dawn gave him a sultry smile, and whispered, "I do remember!" They moved as one, as if the past was only yesterday. They had not lost a step.

In his eyes, Dawn could see the sheer passion and desire he felt for her. In hers, he saw the look of anticipation, of wanting.

After four songs, no words were spoken. Dawn gently took Brent's hand, and led him into the bedroom. They began the ritual of slowly undressing each other, and afterwards, as they lay in each other's arms, Brent whispered, "For 1,001 nights I have dreamt of this, and now my wish is fulfilled." They fell asleep, luxuriating in the feeling of total bliss.

Dawn awoke to the smells of coffee and cinnamon. She slipped into Brent's robe, and followed the scent to the kitchen. To her delight, a fresh baked pan of cinnamon rolls with thick, cream cheese frosting, sat cooling on top of the stove, next to a fresh brewed pot of coffee.

Out of the corner of her eye she caught movement, and saw Brent standing in the meadow that led to the river. With his camera mounted on a tripod, she could tell he was visually framing an image. He pushed down the shutter control and stepped back from the camera. Thirty seconds later, she saw him view the image on the screen, and raise both arms in satisfaction.

Brent gathered his equipment, and began to walk to the house. When he caught sight of Dawn, his breath caught in his chest, and a warm smile spread across his face. His eyes never left hers as he walked towards her.

After placing his tripod and camera on the deck, Brent took both of Dawn's hands in his, and said, "I had to make a visual record of the first day of the rest of my life, and it seemed appropriate that I capture the sunrise. Lover, I will never be the same person I was, last night changed that. To have a fantasy for years, turn into reality, that is far more than imagined, is the most important blessing I have ever received."

Dawn, with a flushed face, quietly answered him, "I knew, all those years ago, that we were right for each other, and it's a blessing that we came together, even though it took almost forever. Last night, I needed to feel desired, beautiful, and fulfilled, and the months of anticipation had built up to a crescendo that came true. I have no way of knowing where our path will lead, but I will always cherish last night." She kissed his hands, and said, "Now can we eat those delectable cinnamon rolls?" Brent laughed, and they went inside, enjoying breakfast, then each other.

After showering, Dawn dressed for her drive home. She explained to Brent that she was looking forward to visiting with Chris later that afternoon, and wanted to touch base with the girls. They agreed to call each other in the morning.

With a final embrace and kiss, Brent watched her drive away, knowing that his heart and soul had never reached the depth of fullness he felt at this moment, and tears of joy stained his face.

Chapter 10

Chris had gone back inside the cabin after visiting with Harry about the lots that were for sale. He made a mental note to call his trustee and inquire about his liquid cash position. He would consider adding these parcels to his holdings.

His mission at this moment was simple, the goal being reflection. Ever since he arrived in Iowa, he had retraced his father's steps, soaking in all the facts and emotions that could possibly be found. The same goal led to more results here, at the cabin. Chris found his heart filled with both regret of never knowing Chet in person, and joy of what he had learned and felt.

In order to save the freshness of the moment, he knew he must accomplish what his father's DNA demanded. To write a poem.

And he began.

Missed, Now Found

I once wrote of the Father I had never met
Imagining all that was missed
By him, by me, by us
His trail, his markers, his thoughts, his words
Now found
Enlightening my mind, my heart, my soul
Fables of a husband who lost one love
First-hand account of finding another
Not as a replacement
But an extension of life's journey
A career of touching lives
Turning a word, a phrase, a sentence
Seeking out that one soul
That you could engage
That you could change
That you could alter their path
And they would alter others
In numbers of ten, one hundred, or more
But your goal remained
One

I found I have your
Eyes, nose, mouth
Mind, thoughts, emotions
Voice, and talent

I felt your touch
On your unpublished novel
Written only for you, and now for me
On the gearshift of your Chris Craft
The doorknob of the cabin
The handle of your rod and reel
The arms of your chair
Where you passed away

And now
I feel
You have found me
You will watch over me
You will guide me
So in the end
They will say
"He was his father's son!"

Chapter 11

Dawn arrived home after noon, and proceeded to do her weekend laundry and catch up on mail. There was a letter from the tenant who farmed the balance of her eighty acres. He was notifying her that he would not be renting her ground for the following year. Dawn felt a sense of relief, she didn't appreciate how the tenant seemed to just take from the soil, never putting anything back. She would have to consider other options for the land. Chris had left a message on voicemail that he should arrive by 5:00 PM. After taking stock of the groceries on hand, she decided to drive into town to pick up supplies for the evening meal with Chris.

Returning from town, she prepared a pork loin roast with carrots, potatoes, and onions, and placed it in the oven. Dessert would be sundaes, using the home-made ice cream she had made the week before. Dawn then toured the grounds, making mental notes about what needed to be done. Her list included mowing, trimming, weeding and watering the garden, and washing all the windows on the outside. She chuckled as she thought, "Oh, the curse of living with a gravel driveway that always creates dust."

At a quarter to five, she heard the crunch of tires on gravel, and ran outside to welcome Chris home. He walked towards her, a big smile on his face, and he said, "I have a lot to talk about, and I am starving!" Dawn told him to wash up, dinner would be ready in fifteen minutes, and she had all the time in the world to listen.

Over plates of steaming mashed potatoes and gravy, fork tender pork, and sweet home grown carrots, Chris began to tell Dawn all he had experienced at the cabin. "First, I would like to thank you from the bottom of my heart for the addition on the back of his headstone. I was overcome with emotion, and felt a sense of validation that I finally belong. I have a connection that can be seen by others. Dawn, that is the greatest gift I have ever been given, and I thank you, again."

Dawn reached across the table to touch his hand as she said, "I know he would have wanted me to arrange that, and it was my pleasure."

Chris continued, "Harry was a great help, guiding me through the nuances of life in the woods. I played your piano, such a rich tone! I found one of his flannel shirts in the closet, and wore it fishing. I discovered his scent and mine are the same. I brought it with me to wash." Dawn interrupted, "That is yours to keep. As a matter of fact, you can have all of his shirts and coats, as long as you leave me one. Sometimes, a girl needs a security blanket. I'm sorry, please continue."

"*Author* is amazing, a work of art in itself. I took it up to the falls, and with the help of Dad's fishing map, I had fresh walleye for lunch. Dawn, his essence is everywhere, from the cabin doorknob, the boat, his fishing tackle, and his shirt. I felt a measure of comfort, kneeling at the grave, somehow knowing that Michelle helped him to his next journey. I can just imagine him looking down at me, then turning to her, and saying, 'That's my son!' with pride. Oh, that reminds me. I wrote a poem I would like to share with you." He pulled it out of his backpack and moved to hand it to her when she said, "Please read it out loud to me."

As Chris began to read *Missed, Now Found*, Dawn closed her eyes, soaking in the tone and timbre of his voice, and as tears began to flow she affirmed Chris was a carbon copy of his father, and she felt blessed that he would share this private, soulful work with her.

When he finished, she wiped her eyes and proclaimed, "Pulitzer Prize Quality!" He, blushing, said, "This one is just for me and you, and Dad."

A silence enveloped the room as they each became lost in their own private thoughts. Chris broke through by asking, "So Dawn, how was your weekend?"

Dawn began to tell him the story of Brent Makenzie from long ago, how he had reconnected with her with a condolence card and check for Chet's memorial. She talked about how Brent was there to help her cope with the loss of Audry, and that last weekend was special, two adults enjoying each other's company. Chris commented, "You seem to have a glow about you, so whatever you did, you should continue it. It definitely suits you!"

With a laugh, she replied, "I will take your advice under advisement, and relay it to Brent. Now, let's build some sinful sundaes!"

Chapter 12

Chris flew home to Portland the following day, and on Saturday, he had a lunch appointment with his mother at her penthouse. Katherine was very pleased to see him, but Chris knew that she would be full of questions about Chet, so he planned to pace himself.

Lunch was served, a delicious combination of thin sliced beef tenderloin combined with mushrooms sauteed in butter, served on a bed of wild rice. An eight-year old bottle of Merlot from their winery was the perfect addition to the meal.

As they began to dine, Chris looked at his mother, smiled, and said, "Why don't I just start and tell you everything?" which she replied, "If you feel you must, I will listen." With a grin, he began, "Dawn was a perfect host. She welcomed me into their home, and was very tender about the situation." Chris reached into his vest pocket and pulled out a large jewelry case, opened it, and said, "She was gracious to present me with this ring and cuff-links. Chet had them custom made years ago, and always wore them when he dressed up. In her heart, she felt that he would want his son to have them." Katherine admired them, saying, "He was the poster boy for the classical look, and he could really pull it off. That was very kind of her to share."

Chris continued, "She showed me photo albums that covered their life, and then she took me into his office where he did all of his writing. Mother, it was incredible. All of his notes and research are there, along with the first and final drafts of each of his novels. There is also one novel that will never be published. Dawn explained to me that Chet had said, 'I have spent my entire adult life writing for others. I am writing this for me.' Mother, Dawn has never read it, yet she had me sit at his desk, in his chair, and she handed it to me, saying, 'It is only fitting that you should be the first person to read it.'"

Chris looked at Katherine and said, "I can't reveal the story to you, but I can tell you the title is *Portland Intrigue*, and the copyright is 1988."

Katherine's eyes began to water, and she gazed out the window, taking in the skyline of downtown Portland. Wiping her tears, she turned back to Chris and whispered, "1988 was the best year of my life, the year that Chet gave me my greatest gift. You. And yes, I do still miss him."

An uncomfortable silence came between them until his mother said, "Please, son, continue. Tell me about the workshop."

Chris began by telling her about the eclectic mix of the participants, female, male, ages from mid-twenties to early sixties, from shy to border-line overbearing. All in all, a very interesting mix that lead to many dynamic discussions, both in class and afterwards at different "watering holes."

Chris had planned ahead, and produced copies of the five submitted poems to share with Katherine. They included *Shadow Step, Sunday Feeling, Display Window, Porch Swing,* and *Portrait*. As he passed them to her, she asked him to read them to her. When he began, Katherine closed her eyes and took a deep breath, opening up herself to absorb the poem's emotions. When Chris had finished *Display Window*, he noticed that his mother was struggling, emotionally. He asked, quietly, what was wrong, and she replied, in a choked-up voice, "I can relate to the end of that poem, where it says, 'That should be me, I want one night with him, a night that would turn into a lifetime of tomorrows.' Son, that is me, and the result is that I think of your father every day. I apologize, please continue."

Chris read the remaining two poems, and went on to share the critiques of his performance written by the students. Katherine laughed, as Dawn had, at the comments made by the middle-aged woman whose comments were, "Listen to his voice for hours, impeccable manners, and easy on the eyes!" Katherine added, "You really are your father's son."

Their conversation then moved to his experiences at the cabin, and when he told her about his name being on Chet's tombstone, Katherine took his hand, and quietly said, "I know all about that. Dawn granted me the courtesy of a phone call, explaining what she wanted to do, and I agreed immediately. Son, if she is as nice in person as she is on the phone, I would love to meet her."

Warning bells began to ring in Chris' mind. The thought of these two woman getting together would be like a 5.5 on the Richter scale, or trying to blend oil and water. He tried to hide his physical shiver as he replied, "Maybe in the future, that would be possible. Now, let me tell you about some real estate."

With those words, Katherine switched into her business persona. Chris explained to her the situation of the two lots that bordered Chet's cabin, and that he had scheduled a meeting for the following month with their accountant and trust officer to discuss the possible purchase of the lots. Katherine wanted to know the reason for the purchase, and Chris replied that, in the future, he might consider building a cabin on one, and by buying the other one, he would be controlling the access to Chet's property.

He went on to tell her about the boat and fishing, but he could tell she was losing interest. He said, "Mother, that is all for today, I need to go home and get ready for tomorrow. I am going up to the vineyard to check out the grape conditions, and make sure the new bottling machine is on line. Thank you again for lunch." He kissed her on the cheek, and after he left, Katherine poured one more glass of wine and moved towards the windows, catching a glimpse of Mt. Hood through the constantly moving fog. And she thought, "I would have given it all up for a lifetime of tomorrows!" And she wept.

Chapter 13

Dawn had resumed her normal routine, with one added feature. There seemed to always be some type of maintenance on the property, from yard work to preparing the outside of the house for painting. The garden had produced record amounts of vegetables, and much to her relief, the Russell girls were masters at canning. They were always volunteering to come to Dawn's on the weekends to help, and each time they left, half of the produce went back home with them.

Dawn was still involved in the Writer's Workshop at ISU, and had been working with Sondra Whitman, Chet's editor, on finding a guest instructor for the following year. Sondra told Dawn, "It will be more difficult to find one next year. The word is out in the literary community about the success of Chris' class, and you and I both know that writers have fragile egos. It would crush some of them that I know if the response of their efforts to teach didn't match up to Chris' results. By the way, what is Chris up to now?" Dawn replied, "I would rather not comment on that. I know he values his privacy, so you will just have to wait for him to contact you." Sondra then asked, "You know what my next question is, right?" Dawn laughed, and replied, "Yes, I am still working on my manuscript, but, remember, you do not get to see it until it's finished." Sondra let out an exhausted sigh and said, "Writers!" They said goodbye, and promised to keep in touch.

Dawn had enrolled three more girls into her writing program, and their assignment for the following year was to document acts of kindness that they participated in, heard of, or witnessed.

One of their first discoveries happened that fall in Story City. Sadie Russell had learned, from her Bible study group, that there were two widows in town who could no longer keep up with their yard work. She called the principal at the high school, and they arranged a plan.

The following Saturday, all of the football team and half of the cheerleaders went to one house, and the marching band and the rest of the cheerleaders went to the other. Armed with mowers, trimmers, and recycle yard bags, the overgrown yards, filled with an immense amount of oak leaves, were returned to their former glory.

Both widows were very grateful, and offered to pay the students. Both groups declined, suggesting that if they wanted to, the ladies could make a donation to the local food bank. Each of them made generous donations, and a simple idea from Sadie turned into the end result of thirty people having a Thanksgiving dinner that they wouldn't have been able to afford, and two beautiful yards in town.

The one added feature to Dawn's routine was Brent. After that first weekend together, they had kept in contact on a daily basis. Each sunset found them on the telephone in long, interesting conversations. Topics covered were what each of them had done that day, weather, religion, politics, and the economy, and always ended in the baring of their souls to each other. Dawn still found his honesty refreshing, and they had been able to be with each other every other weekend at his home. Brent would laugh while he exclaimed, "It's as though I have joint custody of you, and the rest of your life belongs to all the other things you do! But lover, I cherish every moment we have."

He had also become intrigued with the topic Dawn had given the girls, and had been doing research, trying to find a subject that he could photograph.

He ran across a feature that Eric Hanson, a reporter for KCCI, had compiled about a very small town that had a huge heart. In Holmes, Iowa, in 1943, there was a family in town that had no money for Christmas presents for their children. The residents all chipped in, and each of the children in that family woke up to find presents under the tree.

The tradition continued each year. In 2013, the Holmes Christmas Club locally distributed more than $25,000 worth of gifts and money, which included groceries to needy families, checks to all 46 churches, gas cards and scholarships.

Brent began the process of contacting the club members, explaining that he wanted to document their act of kindness through photographs. Plans were made, and Brent was looking forward to working on the endeavor the following year. He explained to Dawn that the project would take a majority of his time next spring and summer, along with his retrospective exhibit that would open at the Norseman

Gallery in June. In their conversation that evening, Brent said, "Dear, in the time before we were together I only had myself to consider when scheduling jobs and events. Now, you are my first priority, so would any of these plans clash with what you had in mind for next year? If they do, I will change them." Dawn replied with a smile on her face, "You are so considerate! Thank you for including me in the decision process. All of your plans are okay with me. Actually, I am considering changes here at home with the farm and the house, so it's probably good that you will be busy." Brent asked, "May I inquire to what changes?" Dawn answered, "Not sure yet, I am rolling some ideas around in my head, and when I get them narrowed down, we will talk." And with that, they said good night.

Chapter 14

While Brent and Dawn were discussing changes in Iowa, there were some definite changes occurring at Black Duck Lake. On the cusp of another winter season being born, there had been renewed interest in the vacant properties that book-ended the Carrington cabin. Ole Swensen, the realtor in Ash Lake, had received a call from Todd Rosein, vice-president of Northwoods Preservation, L.L.C. He said his company was interested in buying both properties that were next to the Carrington cabin. When Ole told him the price, Mr. Rosein agreed immediately, with one condition. He asked Ole to find someone in the area that would tear down the collapsed cabin, and in the spring, seed the vacant spot with native plants and grasses. Northwoods Preservation would pay $10,000 to complete the task. Ole said, "I think I have just the man for the job. Harry Hanson has taken care of the Carrington cabin for over thirty years, and has spent his life in construction." Todd replied, "Please check with him. I assume the abstracts are up-to-date, with no liens on either property?" Ole answered, "That is correct. Todd, when would you like to close the deal?" Todd replied, "I will wire you 10 percent for escrow today, and I will be in your office next Monday at noon to pay the balance and close the sales. If Mr. Hanson agrees with the terms, I would like to meet him at the site at 1:00 P.M., after the closing. Until then."

The phone went silent in his hand, but Ole was grinning from ear to ear. He had figured his commission in his head, and $30,000 would buy the boat that he dreamed of. He wanted to call the dealer immediately, but decided to wait until the deal was done. He did call Harry to inform him of Mr. Rosein's request, and he agreed to meet him at the designated time. Harry then said, "I always figured that Chris Cody, Chet's son, would buy those lots. Guess it wasn't the right time."

The following Monday, a Gulfstream G150 landed at Falls International Airport in International Falls, Minnesota at 10:30 A.M. Two passengers disembarked the aircraft and entered a stretch Jaguar limousine with dark, tinted windows. The limo headed south on Highway 53, and arrived at the Swensen

Realty office in Ash Lake at 11:45 A.M. Todd Rosein exited the limo and entered the office, where, he was greeted by Ole Swensen.

Ole had all the paperwork laid out on a table, and Todd quickly read and signed each piece under the eyes of the notary that the bank had sent over. When they were finished, Todd handed Ole a cashier's check for $450,000, and picked up the abstracts for Northwoods Preservation L.L.C.'s newest acquisitions.

Todd re-entered the limo, nodded at the other passenger, saying, "It's done," and headed to the meeting with Harry at the lake. Upon arrival, Todd instructed the driver to park at the knoll, next to the grave site of Chet Carrington and his first wife, Michelle. He then walked down the hill and met Harry, who led him to the collapsed cabin, where they began to discuss the offer. While Harry explained to Todd how he would remove the cabin debris, a movement up on the knoll caught his attention.

A tall woman, wrapped in a long, expensive looking, blue coat, with long dark hair that was partially covered with a light blue scarf, had left the limo, and was slowly walking towards the grave site. Harry couldn't see her face, it was masked with large sunglasses. He watched as she knelt down and brushed leaves from Michelle's stone, and then she embraced Chet's, kissing it lightly at the top. She then took a piece of paper from her right coat pocket and laid it at the base of Chet's stone. Her body took on the form of someone praying, and then she re-entered the limo.

Harry looked back at Todd, who said, "She is a friend of mine who read all of Mr. Carrington's books when she was younger. When I mentioned where I was traveling to, she asked to come along to visit his grave. She accompanied me last year to Clear Lake, Iowa, so she could visit the spot where Buddy Holly's plane crashed. It's as if she has a bucket list."

Todd then reached into his pocket and pulled out a check for $10,000, made payable to Harry Hanson. He handed it to Harry, thanked him, and walked to the limo that had moved down the hill to pick him up.

After they drove away, Harry walked up to the graves, curious about what the woman had left. He bent down and picked up a piece of yellowed paper. It appeared to be a restaurant ticket, dated 12/10/87. The name was faded, he could make out the first four letters, "Mort", and below were abbreviations with prices, "2fm/mr/$60, 2sal/fr/$20, 2bp/eb/$10, 6gl/mer/$60/ Total/$150.00."

There was a partial signature, and what was left was blurred.

Harry thought, "It must have been important to her, she saved it for over 20 years." He gently laid it back on the stone, placing a small rock on top of it, to keep the wind from blowing away a special memory.

He headed back to his house, check in hand, and began planning how he would finish his new challenge.

Chapter 15

That fall and winter proved to be complex and personally fulfilling for Chris. He had spent much more time than he had originally committed to at the winery. The entire process seemed to mystify him. He worked, side by side, with the migrant workers through the grape harvest. They taught him the technique of picking the grape clusters with no wasted motion, as if it were a science. After a week of toiling beside them, they seemed to open up to him, sharing their life experiences.

To Chris, the gathering of their personal experiences was more important than the crop. Each night he would write in a new red binder, full of lined paper, all that he could recall from the days interactions, and as he closed it when he had finished, he thought, "Dad, I think all these observations will turn into a novel. If not, then the binder will look good on the shelf!"

He religiously kept in touch with Dawn. They had a standing agreement to visit on the phone each Wednesday night right after supper. That would give them plenty of time to share what was going on in their lives, and the call had to end before sunset. That time was reserved for her and Brent.

Chris always felt refreshed after talking to Dawn. She was the exact opposite of his mother, who was always business, while Dawn was about emotion. Chris would smile to think that these two women were his personal source of perfect balance, his ying and yang.

On their previous call, Chris had told Dawn about the news from Black Duck. He explained that, after visiting with his CPA and trust officer, he had decided to purchase the lots on either side of Dawn's cabin. He had called the realtor, and received the news. Earlier, towards the end of fall, a corporate entity had purchased both lots. They had even commissioned Harry Hanson to tear down what was left of the abandoned cabin, and then new white pines were planted in its place. Dawn asked Chris what the new owners name was, and he replied, "Northwoods Preservation L.L.C." They both hoped that the company would live up to its name, preserving the ambiance of the area.

Chris then explained to Dawn that he needed to invest some excess capital, and was thinking of looking at some Iowa farmland. He said he would prefer that the purchase be as close as possible to Dawn's place. Dawn replied, "I would love to have you close to home. If you could wait a month or two, I will check around to see what is available." Chris agreed, and after their call ended, Dawn began to think of the possibilities in her area.

The harvest at the winery was complete, and the nectar of the crush would soon be blended to produce a memory for some young couple in love eight years from then.

When Chris returned home to Portland, he called his mother and suggested, "I would really appreciate it if you would go to the book store and then to dinner with me on Saturday. Would four in the afternoon work for you?" Katherine replied, "What a wonderful idea! It has been so rainy and damp. Finally the forecast is sunny, warm and dry. Let's go outside and enjoy the day. See you on Saturday!"

Chapter 16

While Chris was having his Saturday, mid-morning coffee, he heard the flap of his mail slot open and close. He walked to his foyer and retrieved a single letter that was laid on the ebony marble floor. He went back to his dining table, sat down and took another sip of his coffee. Examining the letter, he noticed the return address was Iowa State University/English Department.

After taking another sip, he opened the letter, unfolded it, and began reading. A broad smile came across his face as he read it a second time. The English Department at ISU had invited him to be a guest professor in the poetry division, starting the following fall, for a term of two years. He would be working with advanced freshman his first year, and would retain the same students as sophomores. The goal was to guide the next generation of poets to "Advance the quality of the written word in poetry, which will enhance the quality of life for humanity." His financial grant would be $160,000, spread out over the 24-month period. An anonymous donor had gifted the funds for this specific arrangement, with a caveat that the opportunity would only be presented to Christopher Cody.

Chris was overcome with joy, his thoughts being, "I will have the opportunity to help young talent evolve into the future of poetry, and I will be walking in my father's footsteps on the campus that meant so much to him!"

He was elated at all the possibilities, and realized that the afternoon's schedule with his mother had just become more interesting. Chris began to steel himself, knowing she would not be pleased at the fact that he would be in Ames, Iowa, and not Portland, Oregon, for two years.

He arrived at his mother's penthouse at 4:00 that afternoon, and after pleasantries were exchanged, they began to walk to Powell's Book Store. It was an unusually warm and dry afternoon for late winter Portland. With imagination, a person could believe that the scent of spring was beginning to fill the air.

While walking, Chris explained to Katherine what he wanted to purchase at the bookstore. His mission was to find poetry books authored by poets from the 1930's to the 1940's. He hoped that he could find the authors Edna St. Vincent Millay, Lorine Niedecker, Robert Hayden, and William Carlos Williams. When his mother inquired as to why, Chris said the reason would make a lively conversation at their dinner later that evening.

As they entered Powell's Book Store, Chris was taken back to his childhood. Here, in this store that covered an entire city block, were all the words that fueled a child's imagination. You could be a cowboy, astronaut, doctor, big game hunter, racecar driver, football or baseball player, explorer, or movie star. Any dream could be matched with a book. He remembered coming here with either his nanny or his mother, finding in the book shelves his escape for that day, and selecting a comfortable chair in a recluse corner of the store. He would always look at the back of the book jacket first, taking in the photograph of the author, and reading the bio. There were times where he imagined his picture there, the dashing, swashbuckling adventurer who survived a potential death-defying ordeal, and lived to write of his escapades.

Then, there was the scent and feel of the book, a combination of ink and paper, once black on white, now fused together in a light gray ink on an ever-so-light shade of ivory parchment. Chris would wonder, "Who was the last person to read this before me? I can feel their fingerprints on the cover, and on each page. Is that the stain of a tear? Why is this page bent over at the corner? Was it important to them? Is there a nugget hidden there that I missed?"

A loud sneeze in the next isle brought him back to present time, and he told his mother he was going to the poetry section, and she informed him she would try to find some new fiction books for her library.

An hour passed as if only a minute, and Chris had found all he wanted, all first editions. He gathered his books and went to find Katherine. On a hunch, he headed to the fiction area, where authors were found alphabetically, and went to the "C's". She was there, sitting in a chair that was pulled up to a Mission style library table. There sat four books in a stack, and one that she was reading. Before she noticed Chris, he saw that all the books were from one author, Chet Carrington.

He sat across from her, and she looked at him, and said, sheepishly, "I had forgotten how well your father could marry words and emotions together to reach heartstrings. God, what a talent! And son, you have been blessed with it, also." She continued, "I am going to buy these to put on the coffee table in the sitting room. I hope you found what you were looking for. Let's go, I am famished!" They paid for their books, and headed out to Morton's Steakhouse.

When they arrived, the maitre d almost stumbled trying to get to them. With a theatrical performance worthy of a "Tony", he gushed, "Katherine, what a pleasure to see you again. You are beautiful, as always!, And Chris, I have been reading impressive things about you in the paper; poet, author, teacher! I have your special table ready as always! Please follow me, and I will have a bottle of your favorite Merlot sent right over."

As they were seated, all eyes caught a glance of Katherine, and just her presence created new fodder for dinner conversation.

Once their wine was poured, the headwaiter came to take their order. Chris said, "Mother, if you would allow me?" She nodded, and he continued, "We would each like a filet minion, medium rare, baked potato, extra butter, and the house salad with French dressing. Thank you."

And before he could ask, Katherine volunteered, "Yes, this is where he and I sat so long ago, and our dinner tonight was the same as back then. Am I that predictable?" Chris replied, "Old habits die hard, Mother. Ever since I can remember, this is what we have always ordered here, and this is where we have always sat. Now I understand."

She interjected, "So, what is the news you are going to tell me?" Chris began, telling her about the unique opportunity at ISU, how he was looking forward to guiding young poets-to-be, and the grant that made it all possible. He explained that the books he purchased at Powell's would form a base line for the development of his class criteria. Katherine listened patiently, and when he paused, she began, in her usual business mode. "I congratulate you on the opportunity, it reinforces what I have known, that you have talent far beyond your years. I think your plan is solid. Why don't you try it here, first, at Portland State?" Chris replied, "Mother, they didn't offer." She lowered the volume of her voice, and replied, "The president of PSU is sitting two tables over from us. I could arrange it in thirty seconds, and it would be done. I would also put up the grant, but I would increase it to $200,000. Deal?"

Chris replied, softly, "Thank you for your support, and generous offer, but this opportunity came to me on my own, and I want to take the chance and build on it. Just think, I will have the responsibility to touch someone's life, and you always taught me that those that have much must deliver more than we take. Bottom line, that is what I want to accomplish."

"I will still have my townhouse here, and you can visit Iowa, you know. I am in the process of looking at land around the area for an investment, maybe I will find an old farmhouse to live in while I am teaching. Mother, I hope you can understand, and be supportive of me."

She reached across the table and covered his hand with hers, and replied, "I will miss your company, but I will always be your cheerleader. You know, I have never been to Ames, it may prove to be a new experience. Now, let's enjoy our dinner." The head waiter arrived, and served their food. After a few bites of the sinfully tender steak, Katherine made a mental note to herself. She would call her attorney when she arrived back home tonight, and would assign him the task to find out who put up the money for the grant that would take her son from her.

Chapter 17

Dawn had spent the past few months soul-searching, trying to make a decision. She and Brent had a routine that was very comfortable, no pressure, and satisfying.

The three girls were doing top-notch work, both in school, and helping their grandmother. The time they spent with Dawn's new bevy of students was helping them form even more good character traits that would serve all of them well in adulthood.

Sondra Whitman had narrowed her search down to two candidates for the guest lecture spot at the next Carrington Workshop. The first one was Slim Warner, a real life cowboy who had built a niche of followers with his unique style of poetry. He had stayed true to the adage, "Write about what you know." A graduate of Colorado State, he had a working cattle ranch in southern Montana that had been in his family for 150 years.

The other candidate was Cheri La Bonn, a writer with an MBA from Harvard. Her parents immigrated in the 1980's, and she was a first-born American. She was a stunning beauty, six feet tall, blond hair, blue eyes, and a figure that had helped her earn enough income as a model to totally pay her college expenses. She was currently an associate editor at a New York publisher, and Sondra had begun the dance of luring her to the Written Word.

The choice was Dawn's to make, but she wanted to have input from Chris. He had set the bar high as the first instructor, and, after all, it was his father's legacy. She had waited to call him. She was just finalizing an important decision that could have an effect on his life, and she was still visiting with Brent about the options that were before her.

She was taking stock of where she was in the moment of life. Her home, the building that was born a corncrib, had housed her life with Chet for twenty years, and had sheltered Michelle for fifteen years before her. They were both gone now, but their essence was still in the night air. The exterior was in need of tender care. Dawn had made the comparison the previous night, when preparing for bed, she noticed her own exterior had continued to change. Those barley visible lines that surrounded her eyes and mouth just five years ago had become prominent features. She laughed as she recalled a quote from Audry before she passed, "You are a vibrant woman, still on the edge of being attractive." Dawn felt that she had finally fallen off that edge, but she was comfortable with that. She had nothing to prove, no one to impress, comfortable in her own skin.

    Brent loved her for what she was now, a confident woman who was satisfied with who she was. After visiting with Brent, she had reached a decision. The home of Chet Carrington needed extensive work, and she was not up to the task. The offer would be made to Chris. Dawn would sell him seventy acres, including the house, office, and pine grove. She would keep the remaining ten acres and build a new house. On the grounds would be a three acre lake, and her new house would have a music solarium that looked over that lake. Her baby grand piano was meant to play only near water, and it would come here from the cabin, for her to enjoy, as the first light of each morning kissed the water, making the surface sparkle like a diamond mine.

    She had elicited a promise from Brent that he would help with the design, including a part of the house that would be his own personal space when he visited. She would leave the physical past to Chris, for him to explore and be absorbed. She was starting fresh, once again.

Chapter 18

Dawn reached Chris the following day at noon. When he answered his phone, she began, "I have looked around for some property for you, and I think I have the perfect parcel for you. It is a seventy-acre tract, just off the two lane road, fifteen minutes from Story City, and twenty minutes from Ames. Sixty-five of the acres are tillable. The other five acres contain a mature white pine grove, a chicken house that was converted into an office thirty-some years ago, and an old corncrib that is now a one bedroom home, but completely modern. I did some digging into the history of this place, and found out that a best-selling author lived here at one time.

Farm land has been selling around this area for $9,000 per acre, on the average. The owner will accept $5,000 per acre, but only from you. So, what do you think?"

Chris was at a loss for words. Two years ago, he had no idea who is father was, and now he had the opportunity to purchase his father's home. The idea of living in the place where his father lived his entire adult life while practicing his craft of writing overcame him. Dawn could hear choked sobs on the phone, and finally Chris whispered, "Thank you, and it is done!" Dawn went on to explain, "You will have neighbors. I am building a new home with a three-acre lake on the other ten acres in the parcel. I will also be planting a new pine grove for future generations to enjoy. I hope that is alright with you?"

Chris laughed, saying, "I wouldn't have it any other way. Now, I have some news!" He explained to Dawn the position at ISU that he was taking, and how the timing was perfect for the land purchase. He continued, "As you know, I have been involved in a winery out here in Oregon, and I plan to plant a vineyard on my new property."

Dawn answered, "Great, now I will know where my Merlot will be grown. So, when will you be arriving?"

Chris answered, "I will see if our company pilot and Gulfstream jet are available tomorrow. If so, I will fly into Ames, and rent a car." Dawn replied briskly, "No way young man. I will pick you up at the airport, you can walk around your new possession, and we will have a home-cooked meal. I insist."

And the foundation of hopes and dreams for two people became a reality.

Chapter 19

Spring arrived in a flurry of activity for all who were associated with Dawn Carrington. Brent had thrown all his talents into the design effort for Dawn's new home. Working hand in hand with her, he had, in the back of his mind, a simple statement that Dawn had spoken during "pillow talk" the past month when she had came for a visit. She had whispered, "All of my life, I have lived in someone else's home. Starting with my parent's house, then college dorms, Audry's house in Westside, then Chet's home and cabin. I hope this doesn't sound selfish, but I think I deserve a place that reflects who I am now, and a vision of who I can become." Brent had nuzzled into her neck while he replied, "I support your feelings 100 percent. You deserve a change. All I ask is that you keep a few square feet for me so I can have a dresser to keep clean clothes in." Dawn laughed, saying, "If you play your cards right, you won't need any clothes!" Followed by, "I can't believe I just said that! You have been a terrible influence on me, and I love it!"

She had finally decided on the house design. It would be a ranch style, with a Mission influence, formed like a large "T". The layout would include two master suites, one on each end, separated by a large open area that would serve as a living room, dining room, large kitchen, and a guest bathroom. The leg of the "T" would stretch out over the first ten feet of the lake, and would serve as her music solarium. Just thinking of her old Steinway there, her fingers blessed by the first rays of morning sun as she opened her soul to her music, gave her goose bumps.

A raised berm would be constructed on the north side of the house, and would be planted with three rows of white pines, thirty in each row, spaced ten feet apart. She could actually hear, in her heart, the wind kissing the boughs, bring forth new memories.

For Chris, his plans for a vineyard were in full bloom. After careful research, with the help of ISU Extension, he had decided on three varieties of grapes. They were La Crescent, Brianne, and Marquette, which would be planted in equal numbers. The first planting occurred that spring, and covered ten acres. The balance of the land was seeded in red clover. The goal was to attract honeybees, and to have a hay crop to sell.

The three Russell girls, Wren, Meadow, and Lark, had been an important part of the planting of the vines. They would stop by after school, and come by on the weekends to help Chris. He had made it perfectly clear that he would keep track of their hours, and pay them once a week at a rate of $20.00 per hour. They all protested, but he was firm, explaining that this was a business, and he would not accept free labor. All three grudgingly agreed, and by the start of school that fall, each one had added $6,000 to their bank accounts.

Wren couldn't wait to arrive at the vineyard as often as possible. She looked forward to the discussions she would have with Chris. Topics were literature, music, and life philosophy. She would tell herself, secretly, "The boys I know at school, and occasionally go out with, are so immature compared to Chris. He is level-headed, soft-spoken, and really listens to my point of view. And I love to see him work with his shirt off!"

Chris and Dawn had decided that she would stay in Chet's house until her new home was finished. He purchased a used Airstream trailer from the dealer in Story City, and had set it up next to Chet's office. This would serve as his base of operation, until Dawn had moved.

To all this activity was added the responsibility of the next writer's workshop. The choice of instructors had been narrowed down from two to one. Slim Warner had called Chris, and explained that, due to the best hay-growing weather in southern Montana in decades, he could not afford to take a week off to teach. Chris told him he understood, and would keep his name in consideration for future years, which Slim thanked him for.

That left Cheri La Bonn as their only choice. Dawn, Chris, and Sondra had a conference call, and based on Sondra's strong recommendation, they agreed to issue an invitation. All three of them were on the call to Cheri, who was thrilled for the opportunity. All the arrangements were made for her travel, and Chris asked her for one favor. "Cheri, would you please write a poem describing yourself. I am interested in your style of writing, and I may want to use your work as an example in the fall classes I am teaching at ISU, if that would be all right with you." She replied, "I welcome the challenge, and will send you one as soon as possible." Within two days, he received this by e-mail.

Myself

Product of two lovers
French born, English raised
Immigrants, now citizens, oath sworn
So I would be first generation
American
Taught that here, all flavors and ingredients
When thrown in the pot
Result in a dish of incredible taste of life
No limit on servings
Father says, "Take your fair share!"
Mother says, "Leave enough for those still to come!"
Sacrifices made by them, for me
Private schools, tutors, valedictorian, summa cum laude
Harvard MBA
Laying my own ground work for my path
I ask, "Don't judge me by my looks, but by what I gleaned from books."
I ask, "Don't look at my figure, but listen to my theory."
A surface is shallow, a drive and desire are deep
I recognize and welcome support
I will lay aside the negative
For in the end, I ask that the truth be said
"She was a model citizen!"

Cheri La Bonn

Chris read the poem several times when he received it, then laid it down for a week. Once he came back to it, he had a clear mental picture of Cheri, and her poem would provide a deep contrasting tool when compared to the masters he would share with his fall class.

It had definitely peaked his interest in her, on a personal level. He decided that he would ask her out to dinner the night before the workshop started.

Chapter 20

A full-blown summer had arrived on the Carrington compound. The spring rains came in perfect amounts, and Dawn's pine trees, along with Chris' grapevines, had soaked up every drop. The construction of the new house was progressing at a record pace. Dawn was very thankful that Brent had set aside his work schedule to act as the managing contractor, and, baring a weather setback, she would be able to move in by the Fourth of July.

Chris was also extremely busy, caring for the vineyard, laying out his course for the upcoming fall semester, and finishing all the preparation for the workshop that would begin in two days. Dawn and he had decided that Chris would give the opening remarks at the welcome reception, introduce Cheri to the attendees, and then disappear. He didn't want Cheri to feel that he was looking over her shoulder, silently critiquing her. He was really looking forward to having dinner with her the following evening.

Cheri was also thinking of the pending dinner engagement. After accepting the offer to teach the workshop, she had done an in-depth study of Chris Cody. She had found that his educational experience equaled hers, his reputation as a poet and author was uncanny for a person of his age, and the list of unexpected kindness done for humanity by him were much more impressive than hers.

She had gathered images of him from the internet, and had reached the conclusion that, on top of all his accomplishments, he was easy on the eyes.

The following evening, Chris picked Cheri up at the Memorial Union on campus. He was stunned by her beauty, the initial reaction on seeing her was "walking perfection". They made small talk as he explained they were going to the Open Flame Steak House in Gilbert, just a few minutes north of Ames. As he drove, he pointed out the Campanile and Morrill Hall to her, explaining the significance of the structures. She talked about what an honor it was to be involved in the workshop, and expressed hope that she could do half as successful as he had the previous year. As he took an inventory of her physical attributes, he commented, "I have all the confidence in you that a stellar performance will be presented." She reached over to touch his hand as she said, "Thank you!" and left her hand on his.

Once they were seated at the restaurant, he explained to her that each guest would pick out their own steak and grill it. Being a new experience for her, she asked him to make the selections. He chose two New York strips, and showed her how to put them on the grill. When they were cooked to a perfect medium rare, they went back to their table where the waiter had delivered their salads and baked potato.

Cheri took the first bite from her salad, then said, "This is not the dressing I ordered." In a raised voice, she called out to the waiter, "Did you not understand my choice of dressing? I specifically asked for French, which this is not. Take this away and bring me the correct one!" The waiter, clearly embarrassed, went to correct the mistake. Cheri looked at Chris, and uttered, "Where do they find these people who are totally incompetent?"

Inside, Chris was fuming. All the good thoughts that he had about Cheri, the potential of developing a relationship, had vanished in a moment. Her rude behavior had shown him the "real" her, and he would not be associated with someone who displayed that attitude. He said to her, in a controlled voice, "To answer your question, the people who work here are college students trying to supplement their income."

The waiter returned with the correct salad, and Chris thanked him. Their dinner conversation slowed from that point on, as if they were just going through the motions of civility. When Chris excused himself to pay the cashier, he found the waiter and apologized for Cheri's actions, adding, " Take this as a solemn oath from me. You will never see her cross your threshold with me, again." He then handed him a fifty dollar bill that was folded, and shook his hand.

He went back to the table and said to Cheri, "You have a busy day tomorrow. We should get you back to the Union." The drive back was silent, and when he dropped her off she suggested they have a drink, and he declined. He wished her good luck, and as he drove home, he thought it would be interesting to see the students' critiques at the end of the session.

The following morning, he had Brent and Dawn over for breakfast, and explained the previous night's experience to them. With a stern look in her eyes, Dawn said, " I will be at the conference on the last afternoon, and will personally have each participant fill out a review on Cheri, and I will collect them. Chris, thanks for the heads-up."

They finished breakfast while they talked of the 4th of July plans. Due to Brent's efforts, Dawn would move in on July first, and a housewarming party would be held on the 4th.

In addition to Dawn, Brent, and Chris, Sadie and the three girls were invited, and Dawn had gone out of her way to invite Katherine. She had graciously accepted, thrilled to see her son, and would be flying in the day before. Chris decided that she would stay in Chet's house, and he would bunk in his Airstream.

As he went to sleep that night, a phrase came into his mind, "Oil and water!"

Chapter 21

The afternoon of July third was definitely not a typical Iowa summer's day. Folks who had spent their lives here knew July would bring high humidity and 90 plus degrees weather. Down at the co-op, the farmers would say, " Good for the crops!" or, "You can hear the corn grow!"

The past week had seen temperatures in the low sixties, with nighttime temperatures in the high forties. Chris had joined Dawn and Brent for afternoon coffee the day before, and Brent, in a deadpan expression, had said, "It's all that damn global warming that Al Gore always talked about. Guess he was right!" They all chuckled. Chris told them that Wren had been working in the vineyard that morning, and had found him in the office. With her hands on her hips, and a defiant look on her face, she declared, "Listen buddy, I do not work outside without a sweatshirt if it is below 70 degrees. The Pioneer Seed thermometer hanging on the shed says it's 58, so, if you want me to work, pony up a sweatshirt now!"

Chris said he could not contain his laughter as he went inside his Airstream and came back with his old PSU sweatshirt. As he handed it to her, she looked at the letters and said, "Really?" and "You are going to teach at ISU, right?" and then, "I guess this will have to do."

They all laughed at his story, but what they didn't know was, when Wren put on Chris' sweatshirt, she was enthralled with his scent. She thought to herself, "This is what his skin must smell like, up close." With a smile of satisfaction on her face, she skipped back to the vineyard to finish the weeding.

Dawn had finished moving into her new home. Chris had spent some time cleaning Chet's house, which was now, officially his home. In anticipation of his mother's arrival, all the carpet had been cleaned, and the linens had been changed. The refrigerator was stocked to his mother's preference, and fresh cut flowers adorned the dining table. Chris decided to stay in his Airstream until Katherine left for Portland.

The long, black limousine pulled into Chris' driveway at 4 o'clock that afternoon. He met his mother after the driver had opened her door, and they enjoyed a mother and son embrace. Upon entering the house, she freshened up, and spent a few moments taking in the ambiance of the place where the father of her child had lived.
    There was a knock at the door, and Chris greeted Dawn. Even though she had talked on the phone with Katherine, this was their first, face-to-face meeting. Chris watched as an observer as the two women sized each other up. There was a polite tension in the air, but, as prearranged by Chris, Dawn suggested to Katherine, "It is such a beautiful day, I would like you to join me for a glass of chilled wine in the pine grove. Chris, I would appreciate it if you would go next door and help Brent set up for supper. I will escort your mother to my home in a short while. Katherine, shall we?"
    As the two women leisurely walked towards the grove, Dawn explained the history of the place to Katherine. "Chet and Michelle came here almost forty years ago. There were two buildings, a chicken house and a corncrib, and this pine grove. They worked hard, turning the crib into their home, and the chicken house into an office. That is where he wrote his books. They spent countless hours here, in this grove, daily enriching their love." She motioned Katherine to sit in the chair that was Chet's, and she poured two glasses of wine that had been chilled in an ice bucket on the table. She continued, "He built these chairs from lumber he found in the corncrib, and you are sitting in the one where he passed away." Katherine had an uneasy look on her face, but Dawn continued, "There are some things I want to say to you, and I thought we should do it in private."
    "When I first found out that Chris was Chet's son, I had a conflict of emotions. I asked myself how a woman could keep a son away from a father, not even telling him of his existence. My original thought was that you were selfish and mean spirited." Katherine began to speak, but Dawn raised up her hand and said, fiercely, "Please, let me finish!" Chastised, Katherine remained mute. Dawn continued, "Many times Chet and I talked about what a shame it was that neither Michelle or I couldn't produce an heir for him, and he would always say that it was destiny. He had all these feelings and emotions of a life lived, and his outlet was his writing. So, instead of sharing it with his child, he shared it with all of humanity."

"I thought you were selfish at first, then I looked inside myself, and found out that I was, also. If you had told Chet years ago about Chris, he and I would never have met. He would have moved to Portland to be near you and his son. I don't think he would have written the books that he did, a man with a family would have had a different slant on life. And I would probably still be in Westside, Iowa, teaching school, and returning to my home each night to dine alone. So thank you for not interrupting my destiny."

Dawn took a long sip of her wine, and continued, "Now, I want to compliment you on the raising of your son. He is as close to perfect as anyone I have ever met. I can't imagine how hard it was for a single mother to raise a child, and be successful in business at the same time. I do understand that you have a tremendous amount of drive, so the way Chris turned out is no surprise. You will always be his mother, but I do love him like a son. Each moment I spend with him reminds me of his father, and I thank you for that. That's all I wanted to say. I hope, for Chris' sake, we can become friends. You will always be welcome in my home. Shall we head to dinner now?"

Katherine had never had a woman talk so honestly to her, and she found it soul cleansing. She asked Dawn, "Do you mind if I sit here for awhile by myself?" Dawn replied, "I understand. Take as much time as you need. When you are ready, just follow the blue slate path that leads from Chris' house to mine." She then walked away, leaving Katherine with her thoughts. The sky had suddenly darkened, and the wind rose through the pine boughs. She thought that it never would have worked, she and Chet. She could have never lived here, in the country, away from all the excitement and stress of business. That is what she had thrived on. And Chris was now learning of his father, living in his home, and using his inherited skills to further the Carrington legacy. Both she and Chet had made sacrifices in life, but in the end, there was their son.

Out of the darkened sky came a single bolt of lightning that struck on the north side of the grove, the wind laid down, and quite calm floated over Katherine. With pain in her heart and tears flowing down her cheeks, she looked up and whispered, "I understand, and I am sorry."

As she gathered up her glass and ice bucket and began to walk to Dawn's house, she wondered, "Is this what church feels like?"

Dawn, Brent, and Chris looked tentatively at Katherine as she approached. She went to Dawn and embraced her, saying "Thank you." And Dawn replied, "Enough said."

Chris introduced her to Brent, and Dawn gave her an informal tour of the house that ended in the music solarium.

As a surprise, Chris pulled out the piano bench, took a seat, and began to play Over the Rainbow. It was a flawless performance, and he noticed his mother's hands fly to her heart as she uttered, "sixth grade music recital at the academy. Thank you for that memory. I do love you, son."

Chapter 22

They all arrived at Dawn's by 5:00 in the afternoon on July Fourth. Sadie and the three girls came bearing baskets of food that included enormous amounts of Sadie's county fair, blue ribbon fried chicken, baked beans, and, it seemed, three gallons of potato salad. Brent and Chris had spent the afternoon slow-cooking racks of ribs on the grill, and Dawn and Katherine had picked fresh green beans and onions, and cooked them with bacon. Earlier in the day, they had gone to the road ditch to pick luscious raspberries, a feat that Katherine said was brand new to her. These were served over homemade ice cream after dinner.

The three girls were in rare form. Wren had washed the PSU sweatshirt, and walking inside when she arrived, told Chris, " I checked. It's 68 degrees. I am wearing it!" He laughed and replied, "Whatever makes you happy." And she thought, "If you only knew."

After dinner and dessert, Katherine inquired about the book that the three girls had written. Dawn, proud as a mother hen, told her that the book was already in its fourth printing, and everyone loved it, especially the publisher. Chris, Brent, and Sadie asked the girls for a reading, and after an act of shyness by all three, they caved to the pressure, and gave an animated reading in the solarium. A round of applause greeted them as they finished, and Katherine asked if she could order 120 copies for the academy where Chris went through the elementary grades. Lark responded quickly, "Will that be a check or credit card, and what address?" Meadow added, "Because of who you are, we will give you a break on quantity discount," Wren acted embarrassed, but Chris said, "It's business, right Mother!"

After completing the transaction, they all moved outside, grabbed folding chairs, and followed the path to Chris' newest edition. He had created a rise at the start of the vineyard, and designed and built a pergola. The curved rafters had a sensual appeal, and on both sides were fresh plantings of pink, white, and red climbing roses. He had planned that within five years, the vines would completely cover the structure, and he could envision it framing the scene of heavy laden grape vines. He explained to the gathering, "If this works out to my satisfaction, we will be able to host wedding parties here in the future. For now, we should be able to see the fireworks from all the surrounding towns."

The weather held, and in the dark of a blue velvet sky, the fireworks showed brightly. After the grand finale, they all made their way back to Dawn's yard and said their goodbyes. Dawn reminded Chris that they had an appointment in the morning, after Katherine left, to review the student critiques of Cheri La Bonn. She embraced Katherine, and reminded her, "My door is always open to you." She thanked Dawn for the kind words and answered, "You may visit me in Portland anytime." Chris put his arm around his mother, and they walked down the blue slate path to his house.

Over a late night cup of coffee, he and his mother caught up on the Portland gossip, both business and personal. She thanked him, again, for including her in the day's activities, and finished by saying, "Dawn is a very special woman. She was exactly what your father needed in that time of his life. Son, I could have never made him happy, but I am overjoyed that you have all these opportunities to learn about him. Now, are you coming home for Christmas?"

He replied that he would come home at Christmas break, but would be spending Thanksgiving in Iowa. She told him to give her two days notice, and she would send the Gulfstream to pick him up. She added, "It is such a luxury to call up my pilot, give him my destination, and fly off. You would be surprised at the places I have been, and the things that I have seen. Well, honey, it's late, and the limo is due at eight in the morning, so I will retire now. Love you!"

As he retired to his Airstream, he said a prayer of thanks that all went smoothly today, and he really felt part of his new, extended family.

Chapter 23

The limousine was right on time the following morning, and Chris said his goodbyes to his mother. He then walked to Dawn's house, and joined her and Brent for coffee. Together, they went over the previous day's events, and all agreed that the food and the company was outstanding!

Brent excused himself, saying he was going to Ledges State Park to photograph the canyon. He explained the morning light was the best to shoot that location in.

After his departure, Dawn looked at Chris and said, " You must realize that it took a lot of courage for your mother to visit here. She and I had a good talk, and I think we will get along fine, in the future. Now, let's review Cheri's critiques."

She pulled out a file of twenty responses, and both of them began to read. When they had finished, they discussed any common threads that were relevant. Some of the quotes were, "Highly intelligent, excellent grasp of the material, dry presentation." "Satisfying to look at, but a lack of emotion on delivery." "Would have liked the instructor to engage more with us, find out our opinions." "There really are two sides to every story. I didn't appreciate the sense that hers was the only valid one." "I appreciate her effort, but I really do possess feelings and emotions that have been in me longer then she is old." "Sometimes we are presented with comparisons and examples that open our eyes, and, thank God, we have the wisdom to decide which are good, and which are BS."

The last comment drew a belly laugh from Dawn as she said to Chris, "It sounds like my old friend Audry was in class. I can just hear her giving that quote. There is not a day that goes by without me thinking of her." So, Chris, what do you think about Cheri?"

After a long, thoughtful pause, Chris began, "This is just conjecture on my part. I think she is a very complex person. I feel that deep inside her soul, she feels the need to excel, being a first generation American. That is an admirable quality, but somewhere in her life, she built a wall to keep people out, to protect herself. Dawn, what I am learning from reading my father's research and books, is that we are only half of a person if we have not been touched by pain and anguish. We need to suffer loss, to have our heart broken, to feel alone, before we can develop a capacity to love, cherish, trust, and give, without expecting anything in return. Only then can we know empathy for our fellow man. I hope that she will realize this before she becomes so set in her ways, that change will be impossible." Dawn looked him square in the eyes, and said, "You have a very old soul, a wise old soul, just like your father. That trait, alone, will serve you well in life."

"I think that we should forward these critiques, along with our observations, to Sondra. I know she is trying to lure Cheri to her company, and out of respect, I feel she needs to have all the input that is available. Do you agree?" Chris nodded yes, then Dawn brought up another subject.

"Women's intuition is very powerful, it enables us to see things that the male species can't. Mine is telling me that Wren is becoming very interested in you. I see how she looks at you when you are working, how she hangs on every word you say. I know you have not encouraged her in any way. I just wanted to bring it up for your sake. Enough said!" His face had turned red, and he replied, "Thank you. I will be cognizant of the situation."

"Dawn, one other matter. Would it be possible for me to go to the cabin before my classes begin. There is such a Zen quality there. I could clear my head so I will be ready for my students. Also, would it be all right with you if I invited Brent to come along. I feel he is like the older brother I never had, and I would like to spend some time with him." Dawn replied, "You may use the cabin whenever you like. Just let me know, and I will call the Hansons to let them know."

"As far as Brent, you will just have to ask him. Please don't feel slighted if he politely turns you down. I think he still has a few issues dealing with your father's shadow. And yes, it is intuition!"

Later that evening while Chris was checking the drip irrigation lines in the vineyard, Brent sauntered over with two bottles of beer in his hand, and offered one to Chris. Brent grinned at him, then said, "Dawn tells me you will be going to the cabin before school. I think that is a great idea, you can recharge your batteries before they are taxed by youth and the quest for knowledge." Chris laughed, and replied, "I was wondering if you would join me, I hear the walleyes are biting."

Brent took a long pull off his bottle, looked at Chris, and began, "I really like you, you're a decent young man, and if it was anybody else's cabin, I would be all in. I have nothing against Chet, the few times we met, he was a complete gentleman. But, Chris, he and Dawn have a long history at that place, and I would be conscience of it all the time I would be there. I would just as soon not go there, physically and emotionally. I appreciate your offer. Now, any time you want, you can come up to Lanesboro and stay at my home. We could ride the bike trails, they are beautiful in the fall, next to the river, and best of all, there is not a hint of lingering family history there! So, do you need any help with these lines?"
	Chris said he would welcome the company, and the two of them checked all the lines in the vineyard, finishing right at dark.

Chapter 24

Chris had made arrangements with Dawn and Wren in regards to the vineyard. He had asked them to check the sensors once a day on the drip irrigation lines, to make sure all was good. He didn't want to worry while he was at the cabin, and he knew the vineyard was in good hands.

Harry Hanson met him when he arrived, and opened up the cabin and boathouse. Once he had put his groceries and clothes away, Harry asked if he could show him what had been done on the two adjoining properties. Chris agreed, and they began to walk to the south lot.

Harry told him how he had demolished the old cabin that had been there for ages. He had salvaged most of the wood, it was cedar, and still in good condition. The footings had been removed, and in the footprint of where it had stood were three-foot white pines, planted in clusters. Throughout the rest of the lot, all the invasive vegetation had been removed, and it now resembled a slice of perfect, northern Minnesota virgin land.

As they walked to the north lot, Chris admired at how Harry had changed it. It was now a mirror image of the south lot, in reverse, with the same number of pines, planted in the same configurations of clusters. Harry commented, " The gentleman from Northwoods Preservation L.L.C., Todd Rosein, has been great to work for. He approved all of these plans in twenty-four hours, sent checks immediately. I sent him photographs of the finished project, and kind of danced around the question of what the long term plans were, and he politely answered, "Harry, what you see is the end result, but hopefully, each year, the trees will grower larger. My company is only interested in preserving the land as it should be. One day, in the future, a young couple in love will stop here and simply enjoy the scent of the pines, soak in the music of the wind, gently caressing the boughs, creating symphonies that will never be replayed, always original. And with God's grace, and a little luck, they will experience the Northern Lights, painting the sky on a cold winter night as they lay wrapped together in a sleeping bag, shivering from the sound of a lone wolf, calling its mate. Harry, if that scenario ever happens, then all of your work and my investment were worth it."

Chris had closed his eyes, imagining what Harry had just said, and thought, "I hope I have a chance to live out Mr. Rosein's dream."

He spent the rest of the afternoon just soaking in the surroundings. After a light supper of soup and salad, he poured a fresh cup of coffee, and headed up the knoll. When he arrived at the grave site, he knelt down and swept the fall's first offering of leaves away from the tombstones, then took a seat in the perfectly manicured grass. He began to talk, out loud, to his father.

"Dad, so much has happened since I was last here. A company bought the lots that border your cabin, but don't worry. They did a magnificent job returning them to their natural state. I know you would love the result. By the magic of destiny, I was asked to teach a poetry class at ISU for the next two years. What an opportunity to touch people's lives, and I am sure I will receive back from my students more than I will be able to give. I have learned, by doing research in your office, that is the "Carrington Way!"

I now live in the home that you bought, so many years ago, with Michelle. What a vision you both had to turn a corncrib into a home, and a chicken coop into an office. I wonder if the locals ever talked about it, you know, "That young girl vet and the guy who teaches English down at the college are living in a corncrib. Do they have shelled corn for brains?" He laughed at the thought of such a conversation. He continued, "Dawn was gracious enough to sell me seventy acres, which included your house and office, and most important of all, the pine grove, the hallowed place where you took your last breath. Dad, I have spent hours, sitting in your chair, feeling our connection." Chris wiped the just formed tears from his eyes and forged on.

"Dad, my long term goal is to have a successful winery. There are ten acres in new grape vines now, and each year I will add more. Dawn kept the other ten acres and built a brand new home for herself. She even added a music solarium to house her Steinway, the one that was here, in your cabin. It does sound marvelous, since it is suspended over a body of water. Dawn said that is the way it has always been with her piano. Something about the 'flow of water.'

Anyway, I am spending a few days here recharging my batteries, and planning my fall class. I will be taking *Author* out to some of your secret walleye holes, and enjoying the religious experience called nature. Peace be with you and Michelle. I love you, Dad."

He got up slowly, and kissed his finger, then touched the letters on the tombstone. He had the kind of sleep that night that had escaped him for months. For the next three days, the walleye bite was on. Chris had fish for lunch and dinner each day, and froze his limit to take back to Dawn.

With a fresh perspective for teaching, and a cleansed soul, he bid his father and Michelle, along with Harry Hanson, farewell, and headed south, a 456 mile drive, to his next life experience.

Chapter 25

The fall term came at Chris like a cyclone, spinning him in many different directions. Before his twenty-two students arrived for their first day of class, he had to fill out an immense amount of paperwork for the college administration.

There was an employee handbook to digest, and a class to attend that specifically laid out the ground rules on how a professor should act towards his or her students. The university hosted a cocktail party for all the new educators on the Saturday evening before classes started. The room was filled with newbies like Chris, and at the other end of the spectrum, teachers who had twenty plus years in the trenches at other institutions, who were bringing their expertise to ISU.

Les Brighton was in that category. She had arrived at ISU after twenty years of teaching that spanned time at Missouri, Creighton, and the University of Iowa. Her specialty was psychology, and her position at ISU was head of the department.

She had been divorced for fifteen years, had no children, and had thrown herself into her career. Little of her time was spent in personal relationships in the past. Now, with prestige and financial security, she had planned to have a deeper focus on personal relationships.

Her physical attributes had held up through the years. Dark brown hair, brown eyes, skin that always looked tanned, and a silhouette that would be described as full-figured, all carried on a five and one-half foot tall frame.

Within the first fifteen minutes of the party, she had narrowed down her possibilities to one person. With a drink in hand, she moved slowly across the room, making eye contact with him. When she arrived, she held out her hand, and said, "Hi, I am Les Brighton, the new department head of psychology." He took her hand, and said, "Nice to meet you. I am Chris Cody, and I am a visiting professor here on a grant to teach poetry." Wanting to keep him engaged, so she could study his body language, she replied, "I find poetry a tool to sooth my soul. My favorite is Edna St. Vincent Millay. Her depth of emotion is incredible!" With a smile, Chris answered, "How ironic! She is one of the poets that my students will be exposed to in forming a base line for the comparison of modern poets. They will also be reading Williams, Hayden, and Niedecker, all from the 1930's. And Les, I will be learning right along side them."

As he took a sip of his drink, she was filing information in her brain. "Self-assured, soft-spoken, highly intelligent, great eye contact, handsome, dapper dresser. In other words, the complete package. She asked, "If you don't mind me asking, how did you end up here, at ISU?" He replied, " My home base is Portland, Oregon, but I had the unique opportunity a few years ago to be the guest lecturer at the Chet Carrington Memorial workshop for writers, here at ISU. Evidently, someone liked my work, and invited me to accept a grant to teach here for the next two years. Now, I think it's only fair for you to tell me the same, how did you come to be the head of the Psych department?"

She went on to explain her journey from an undergraduate at Missouri, to an associate professor at Creighton, to full tenure at Iowa, and the unique opportunity here to head a department. She added, "Only 23 percent of department heads in universities across America are female, so I consider myself blessed." Chris replied, "Well, congratulations. If you would excuse me, I am going home to finish my prep for Monday. It was very nice to meet you, and after the semester is underway, we could meet for coffee at the Union, if you would like."

With her best seductive smile, she said, softly, "I will look forward to our next meeting. Here is my card with my home, office, and cell numbers. And Chris, it was very enjoyable meeting you!"

As he began to walk away, her thoughts were, "He has potential."

Chapter 26

Before the fall term began at the high school in Story City, the three girls, along with their grandmother, had invited Dawn over for lunch to discuss the course options available. As they had matured, more interests had come on the horizon. Lark was into sports, and was on the varsity softball team. She had taken an interest into physical therapy after watching the school trainer for the past few years. The kids just called him "Doc Brad", and he had been at the high school for twenty years.

Lark had noticed how "Doc" seemed genuinely concerned with all the athletes when an injury occurred, and his passion was to get them back to normal as soon as possible. He always had a smile of satisfaction when one of his patients took the field, completely healed.

Dawn told Lark that sports medicine was a noble profession, and she, along with Sadie, had steered Lark into courses that were in science and math. They wanted to make sure all her required studies would be completed before college.

Meadow had shown an interest in photography at an early age, and her interest had turned into her passion. She had even mustered up the courage to have Brent critique her portfolio. He was kind, but honest, praising the work that was good, and giving her tips to make the other work better.

After the discussion with Dawn and Sadie, she chose a photography unit, combined with art, and a communication class that included a unit in speech. Brent had said earlier, "Meadow, you will have to know how to carry yourself and get your point across when you are sharing your art with the public. Do they have a class in school that teaches how to grow a thick skin? Believe me, you will need one when an uninformed knuckle-dragger comes up to you and says, "This is what you should have done!" Wren had set her sights on horticulture. To her, the sweetest scent in the world occurred when she would reach down in freshly turned soil, grab a handful, and bring it to her nose. The mystery of growth was contained in those ebony colored particles that, when tossed into the wind, would spread onto countless acres.

Maybe it was because she came from a long line of farmers, dating back through several generations. They were the souls who fed their families, and eventually, fed the world. She knew it was in her blood, it had reared its head when she began working in Chris' vineyard. The self satisfaction of watching a mere wisp of a plant develop into a sturdy structure, its leaves and stems reaching towards the sun, bringing life to itself. Planting a seed that would sprout, then grow, eventually bearing nourishment for its caregiver.

Wren had done her research, and found out that ISU had a course in viticulture, the science of growing grapes, and courses on wine making. That was her goal, and in her heart, she would dream, "I could be closer to him!"

With Sadie and Dawn's input, Wren designed a plan to have all the correct classes for her junior and senior year that would lead to her admission to ISU.

Chapter 27

Fall was a busy time for publishers. Sondra Whitman and her company, The Written Word, were working feverishly to produce titles that would be the best-sellers for the holiday season.

Dawn had sent Cheri La Bonn's critiques to Sondra, along with permission to release them to her. After reading them numerous times, Sondra called Cheri and asked her to come to New York for one more interview. She accepted, and the following week, they met in Sondra's luxury suite of offices. Sondra welcomed her, and said, "I have the critiques from the students at the workshop you taught. Dawn sent them to me, since I was the one who recommended you for the position. Please take a few minutes to read them, and then we will have a discussion." She handed them to Cheri, and watched her facial expressions as she read through them. Her instinct told her there would be no change, no embarrassment, no heat of anger, no indignation. She was right.

When she had finished, Cheri handed them back to Sondra, and said, "Interesting opinions, and in America, everyone is entitled to one, but we do not have to agree. I stand by the way I taught the class. It seems that I took some people out of their comfort zone, and that was my intent."

Sondra was content with that answer, and she said, "I am going to offer you a position here, working with me. I respect your toughness. Believe me when I say it took a lot of pain and pure drive to get to where I am today. You will be editing fiction books. I want you there because I know you won't become involved with the plot line or the characters, or even the emotional aspect of the story. Your final analysis will answer one question, 'Will people buy this book?' That is what I will pay you to do."

Sondra had written a dollar amount on the back of her business card that would be Cheri's yearly salary. She slid it across the table to her, and waited, silently. Two minutes passed, then Cheri stood up, came to Sondra, stuck out her hand, and said, "I accept. Thank you for the opportunity. She then turned and left the office.

As she watched Cheri leave, Sondra thought, "I wanted cold and clear, and that is exactly what I got."

Chapter 28

By the time Thanksgiving break arrived, Chris had already become settled into a comfortable routine. He taught class on Monday, Wednesday, and Friday, from ten till noon, and had open office hours on Tuesday and Thursday from three to five in the afternoon. His students were shy at first about coming in on those days, but they all learned that it was a place of rejuvenation, where ideas about poetry, and life in general, could be exchanged, and there were no wrong answers. After the word got out around campus and on social media, students who were not enrolled in Chris' classes began to show up and interact with the assembled group. Even the administration became aware of his popularity, and Chris was labeled a rising star.

His schedule allowed him to have ample time to tend to his vineyard, and to get his home ready for winter. This was all new to him. In Portland, the building manager took care of any problems at his townhouse, all Chris had to do was call. Here, at the Carrington house, it was all sweat equity. He would always, with grace, turn down offers to help from Dawn, Brent, and the girls. He wanted to savor the experience by himself.

He had also developed a friendly relationship with Les Brighton. Their schedules allowed them to have lunch together on Wednesdays, and a standing date for coffee on Fridays at three in the afternoon. They both enjoyed the conversation, and were slowly building a mutual trust for each other. He sensed that she wanted to take the next step towards intimacy, but Chris wanted to take more time. He had never been one to have casual sex, no one and done. If he would open up to Les about his philosophy on this subject, he thought she would deduce he had buried tendencies caused by growing up without a constant father figure, or a repressed feeling of growing up with a domineering mother. He would laugh to himself about this, and would think, "How many sessions would that take?"

Deep inside, he knew there wasn't that feeling, the feeling of catching his breath each time he saw her, having her be the last thought on his mind before sleep, or the first thought upon awakening. For the moment, he was comfortable with their situation. It was safe.

Thanksgiving Day proved to be another new experience for Chris. He had declined an invitation from Brent and Dawn to spend the day in Lanesboro, and an offer to eat with Sadie and the girls at their large, four-square, farm house.

He wanted to experience the day as his father did, four years after the death of Michelle. In Chet's unpublished novel, *Portland Intrigue*, he had written about his Thanksgiving Day. He had cooked a single turkey breast, made mashed potatoes and gravy, a green bean casserole, and a pumpkin pie. He had opened a bottle of his favorite wine, and enjoyed his personal feast, while taking stock of his place in life. He wrote of a slowly diminishing pain in his heart, and an ember of hope that had begun to warm his soul. He had finished the day by putting on an extra, red flannel shirt, and eating his pie with a steaming cup of fresh coffee, in his chair, at the pine grove.

It was Chris' quest to duplicate the exact same experience, to understand the emotions his father felt on that day, to see if they could make another father-son connection.

At the end of the day, while eating his pie and drinking hot coffee in the grove, clothed in his father's red flannel shirt to ward off the November chill, a turtle dove gently landed on the chair where first Michelle, then Dawn, sat, and sang his lovely song.

With tears slowly moistening his cheeks, Chris raised his head to the sky, and said, "And a happy Thanksgiving to you, Dad!"

Chapter 29

The class assignment was simple, yet challenging. Each of Chris' students had to compose an original poem. There was no single topic. Chris had explained to them, "This one poem will be 50 percent of your grade, and I will give you some free advice. When you have finished it, lay it down. Don't look at it for 48 hours. Then read it, one last time. If it still conveys the emotion that you had planned, if it delivers the message you wanted to share, sign your name, proudly, at the bottom, and turn it in to me. All poems must be in my office the day before winter break. No excuses, and if you do not submit one, you will not be allowed back in class in January. Good luck!"

The poems began to filter in at a snail's pace, until the last day, when Chris was hit with an avalanche of submissions.

When he received the last one, he laughed, and said, "Writers!"

He put them all in his brief case, not reading any. His plan was to drive to the winery in Portland after he stepped off the Gulfstream jet, and read them in the solace of the country.

Before he left from Ames, he and Les had a romantic dinner at her home, where Chris had given her a rare, signed, first edition of a volume of poetry by Edna St. Vincent Millay.

She was thrilled, and kissed him full on the mouth. As he gently pulled away, he said he had an early flight in the morning, and he would see her again when classes resumed.
As he walked to his car, he thought, "Is it time to tell her we have no long range future, or do we just continue to be friendly companions?"

His jet was waiting for him in the morning, and four hours later, the limousine picked him up and delivered him to his home.

He called his mother's office and left word that he was home. They were scheduled for lunch the next day, and he would be leaving for the winery in the afternoon.

Chris had packed a bag with his old work clothes, grabbed his briefcase, and drove to his mother's. She greeted him warmly, and Chris noticed that copies of all of Chet's books were now prominently displayed on the coffee table in the living room. His mother had laid out an elegant luncheon spread, smoked salmon with a pasta side, and strawberries drizzled with chocolate.

Their conversation included all the things that Chris had done since school started, and Katherine informed him of her newest acquisitions. Together, they decided which charity to fund before Christmas, and the Portland food bank was chosen.

After lunch, Chris left for the winery, promising his mother he would be back to spend Christmas Day with her. His drive was relaxing, and, to his amazement, Mt. Hood stood out in clear skies in the distance. He chuckled to himself, "December, in Portland, sunny, and clear skies. What a visual treat!" He finally arrived in the valley where the winery stood. It seemed that the entire enterprise had begun a winter slumber. The harvest had been a record breaker, and all of the grounds and buildings looked pristine. He went to his small apartment that overlooked the winery. From a side window he could see row after row of golden oak barrels that held the promise of a luxurious wine eight years in the making. That was one thought that intrigued him, the fact that there was always next year's vintage to taste, to savor, to mark special occasions with. That was the romance of wine making.

He changed into his work clothes, and started to walk between the rows of vines that stretched before him. There remained a subtle fragrance of ripe grapes in the air, and the therapy it provided put him in a state of sublime relaxation. As he sauntered back to his room, he knew he was ready to give the poems the attention they deserved. With a freshly brewed mug of hot coffee within his reach, he began.

Two hours passed, and he was elated with his students' attempts. The poems touched a variety of subjects, and each contained a measure of emotion. After re-reading them, he selected three that he would read out loud on the first day back at class. These would be the grade "A" poems, the remainder receiving "A-."

He left those three on his table, and put the rest back in his briefcase. After going to town to have a light supper, he returned, and read the three one last time, and was satisfied.

Destination

Six months after birth, we start
Two hands, two knees
Pushing up, moving forward
Discovering the next object with in reach
Graduating to upright, balanced on two legs
Moving forward through life
Head held high, gathering in our surroundings
For decades
Then, a subtle change begins
Slightly curved forward, attention on what is directly ahead
Balance becomes suspect
The gait begins to slow, a cane is introduced
Four turned into two, turned into three
On bended knee, we see
Open arms that display scars on both wrists
Where stakes were placed to fasten Him
On a cross
Tender fingers that beckon
"Come to me
you will be free
from pain."

Flying By

With Grandma's quilt in hand, she walks
South of the barnyard
Counting wooden posts
23, 24, 25 to find
The spot, dug by the fox
His secret passage into the hayfield
On her back, wiggling through, under the wire
There, a perfect spot, alfalfa in bloom, warmed by the sun
Quilt spread, laid down, face up, to see
White, fluffy, floating clouds against a robin egg blue sky
She sees a fluffy poodle, a man with a soft white beard
Cotton balls, locomotive, a running horse, a long fingered hand that turns into a flag, waving in the wind.
Smoke from a chimney of a large white house
Even a giant, large eared, white mouse
Now, all wind swept away, to return another day
She gathers her quilt, knowing that tomorrow
A new cloud will appear
Feeding her imagination
Flying by, in life

Truth?

We have heard these phrases
"Across a croweded room"
"Love at first sight"
"When I looked into your eyes, I knew"
Are they true?
Did they happen to you?
When you first laid eyes on him
Did you gaze as he spoke?
Did they laugh at his joke?
Moving closer to see
The color of his eyes, the jut of his chin
The smile that warmed you
Moving closer, so close
Skin almost touching
Leaving a small space, enough space
For the width of a breath to pass between
Leaving a spark that ignites the feeling in your pulse
As if it were his
Then your eyes meet
And all around, both of you, is out of focus
Out of mind
All that matters is what you see at that moment
And then you will know
The truth

Chapter 30

The time that Chris spent with his mother during winter break was more relaxing than it had ever been before. It was as if she finally viewed him as an equal adult, a person who could successfully navigate his journey without her input.

Or maybe, there were no more secrets to protect. All the truths had been laid on the table the past several years, and they could finally know honesty between them.

After he returned from the winery at the foot of Mt. Hood, the weather turned typical. It brought to his mind the opening paragraph from his father's novel, *Portland Intrigue*, "Rain. Cold. The kind of cold that sinks into every muscle and bone in your body. Day after day, after day, until it sinks into your soul."

He had decided to fly back to Ames a few days earlier. He explained to Katherine, "In Iowa, there is snow, then cold, but, most of the time, the sun does shine. In one's mind, you can imagine warmth. But Mom, you know what it is like here in Portland." She laughed, and responded, "Son, why do you think we always flew to the condo in Hawaii right after Christmas! Now let me call our pilot and schedule your flight to Ames. As soon as he returns from Ames, I will be leaving for the sun and surf." The arrangements were made, and Chris would leave at first light. His driver would take him to the airport while Katherine finished her packing. They said their goodbyes, and made tentative plans for her to visit Iowa in June.

As the jet touched down, Chris took note that the covering of snow that had blanketed Iowa when he left had disappeared, leaving a brown hue on everything. He thought, "One day closer to Spring. Just pulling into his driveway off the two-lane road left a lump in his throat as he thought, "I am home!"

He unpacked, changed clothes, and took a walk through the vineyard. He could imagine that, in a few short months, the vines would be green with leaves, and the small clusters of fruit would be showing.

On impulse, he got back in his car, and drove to Ames. His first stop was at the Campus Florist, where he bought a spring bouquet. He then drove to Les Brighton house, and had to wait as another car was leaving her driveway. The driver looked familiar to Chris, but he couldn't put a name to the face. He parked the car, then walked to the front door and rang the bell. Before the door opened, he heard her voice say, "Don, did you come back for more of me?" Upon opening the door, she suddenly had a look of shock on her face that went in tow with her disheveled hair and opened blouse. She blurted, "Chris, I didn't expect you for four more days, you probably should have called." Suppressing a laugh, Chris replied, " I wanted to surprise you, and I believe it worked."

She asked him to come in, and he declined, saying, "You owe me no explanation, we had no rules to follow, and I hope you are happy. I am sure we will see each other on campus, and if you would like, we could still have an occasional coffee. But that is all. Enjoy your evening."

After starting his car, he began driving, and the farther he drove, the harder he laughed. After his laughter began to subside, he said, out loud, "Dad, I think they call that "dodging a bullet!" He realized she had needs, but Chris was not the one to fulfill them. No one was hurt, and a lesson was learned.

He pulled into the Mary Greeley hospital lot, parked his car, and went to the admission desk. When the receptionist asked, "May I help you?" he replied, "I have a beautiful bouquet of flowers that would look great on your counter. Have a nice evening!" He then left, and she smiled at the act of kindness that was just given to her at random.

Chapter 31

The second semester had started, and all of his students returned with a renewed sense of vitality. Chris had read the three poems he had selected to the class, and together, they had analyzed them. By dissecting each one, line by line, the class learned about the emotional content that went into the process, and all of them knew they would be better poets in the end.

As soon as the frost had left the ground, Chris began to plant the next five acres of his vineyard. He was still impressed by the scent of fresh turned soil, and enjoyed the feeling of honest manual labor. The three Russell girls would show up on weekends to help, and Dawn, and Brent, when he was in town, would always throw a communal style dinner for all to share. Chris enjoyed the simplicity and the generosity that was on display. There was never a hidden agenda.

He had noticed that Wren had changed. Her eighteenth birthday would be in June, she had been offered a full-ride scholarship by ISU to study horticulture following her senior year at Story City, and her body had begun to fill out. He would notice, as she worked along side of him in the vineyard, that the gangly teenager had turned into a beautiful young woman, and he thought she would break her share of hearts.

For Wren, this time of blooming brought on a new set of questions. She didn't feel comfortable talking to her grandmother, Sadie, about it, so she worked up her courage, and approached Dawn when classes were over in June. Dawn asked her over to lunch on a Wednesday, telling Wren they would have the house to themselves.

When Wren approached, she heard beautiful piano music drifting through the opened solarium windows, and that eased her trepidation. Dawn greeted her with a warm smile and a tender hug. She then escorted her into the kitchen. Lunch was BLT's with chips and iced tea. They had informal chit-chat about Wren's schooling, her summer plans, and her work in the vineyard. They moved to the solarium to enjoy turtle sundaes, and after an uncomfortable silence, Dawn suggested, "Honey, I may not have all the answers you are looking for, but I won't know until you ask the questions. I am here for you, and what we say will not leave this room. So, go ahead."

Wren took a deep breath, then began, "I am going to be eighteen soon, I will be in college next year, and I think I love someone who doesn't notice me. All the boys in school are still just kids, big kids. They all put up a front, trying to impress the girls, but deep inside, they are as unsure as we are. Dating is done in a group, not one-on-one, and there is not one that I would go out with by myself. So, here is a question, how do you know if you have fallen in love, and what do you do about it?"

Dawn took Wren's hand in hers, and began, "When I got my first teaching job, I was so lucky to move in with my dear friend, Audry." Wren quipped, "Yea, I always liked her. She was a straight shooter!" Dawn smiled, and continued, "We would have these heart to heart talks about men and love. She would say, "You can't force it, you can't rush it. If it is destined to be, it will happen. All you can do is pray, and remember, sometimes the answer is no." One summer, when I was home in Burlington, playing piano at a restaurant, I met a wonderful man. My mom and Audry would ask me when I came home each night "Frog or prince?" Well, he was a prince, I wanted him, but the timing just wasn't right. Later, I was blessed by meeting Chet Carrington, and we had a wonderful life together.

After Chet died, I thought I was done with men, I had a perfect marriage, and I was content with just living out my life with memories, tucked in the corners of my heart. But then timing and destiny matched up perfectly, and the prince I met over forty years ago, came back to me." With a quizzical look on her face, Wren asked, "Brent was the prince?" Dawn replied, "Yes, honey, he was, and still is. I don't believe we will ever marry, but we have each other, and that is more than enough.

So, the timing for you and Chris hasn't matched up yet, but don't give up hope. You both have years to figure it out. He is still learning about his father, and is not ready to have his emotions directed in a different way." Wren's hands had flown to her face as she gasped, "How did you know?" Dawn laughed as she said, "Women's intuition! Now, you just be yourself, that's all you can do. Live your life, and be happy with your heart and soul. And pray."

Chapter 32

The time for the annual writer's workshop had arrived, and the guest instructor would be Slim Warner, one of the finalists from the previous year.

After meeting with Dawn, it was mutually decided that she would introduce Slim, and monitor the classes. Chris had made arrangements with the Russell girls to watch over the vineyard while he made his way to his much loved visits at the cabin. Wren had said, "Someday, I would like to see what keeps pulling you there." While Lark quipped, "We stay and work, while you go play. What is wrong with this picture?" Chris replied, "All in good time!" to Wren, and "Life has lessons. This is one!" to Lark. They all laughed, and all three thought of the different possibilities.

Chris was packed and ready to leave at first light. Before he turned in for the night, he read Slim's poem, again.

Riding Fence

I walk towards the stable
In early morning light.
He hears the heels of my worn down boots scuff the gravel,
And he snorts, the air from his nostrils forming small clouds.
He knows today is that day. The day after Ash Wednesday
The day we ride the fence.
Each year, for three generations, on this ranch, it marks the coming of spring, the coming of new life.
I lead him out of his stall, this buckskin, strong and tall.
From the tack room comes my Gramps saddle
Given to my Pop, who gave it to me.
Scared leather, still soft and rugged
Images of rosettes, hand tooled on the
Fenders and pommel
Our brand, Flying W, on the cantle
I throw on the blanket, then the saddle
Cinching it up tight.
Then the bridle, that he always fights, tossing his head,
Side to side. Three times
Then stills, as I stroke his black mane.
Pliers and clips in saddle bags
Canteen slung on the horn
My left foot in the stirrup, hoisting up on the seat.
We begin the long ride to the high pasture
Where mama cows and frisky calves will summer
In grass that will tickle their bellies

And the creeks will run cool and clear
I check mile after mile of fence
Tightening the barbs to keep mine in
Tossing aside last years tumbleweeds
Catching the first scent of this years sage
Years ago, I asked my Pop, "Why today?"
He tipped back his sweat-stained Stetson hat
Looked me square in the face, and said,
"Your gramps said it was like a religion, this
Fence riding. So son, that's why we do it the day after Ash Wednesday. Just like he did."
He pulled his hat back down, and said, "Let's ride."

Chapter 33

The trip to the cabin was perfect therapy for Chris. Being engulfed in the nostalgia that surrounded him served as an anchor for his life. He made nightly visits to the grave site, filling in his father and Michelle with all that was new in his life.

On this trip, he had convinced Harry Hanson to take a day off, and together, they took *Author* upstream to where the falls dumped clear, cold water in Black Duck. The walleye bite was on, they had to sort through their catch to keep only the sixteen inch length ones to eat, and put back the others. The two men talked about winterizing the boat and cabin, and Chris told Harry how much Dawn appreciated all he had done for her. Harry waved it off, saying, "I was just doing my job for Chet."

The two lots that Harry had planted for the preservation company looked beautiful. Thanks to Harry's watering, the pines had doubled in size. An image flashed through Chris' mind. He saw himself, wrapped in a sleeping bag with a redhead, sharing the beauty of the Northern Lights as the wind played a symphony in the pines. He shook his head, and got back on focus.

When Chris returned home, he knew he had six weeks to finish all the hard work at the vineyard, and he made a special effort to tell the girls how much he appreciated their efforts while he was gone.

Finally, the fall term started, and all of his original students, who came in as freshman, had returned for their sophomore year. They would spend their entire year polishing their craft, and all of them would enter a poem in the National Poets Contest. With permission from the Dean, Chris had arranged to have a poetry reading, open to the public, each Wednesday night in the Memorial Hall at the Union. Each of his students was required to read one poem every fourth Wednesday, and the event soon became very popular, especially with the sorority crowd.

Chris had started to consider his options. His grant would expire at the end of the academic year, and he knew he must make some long term plans. He had already fielded some unsolicited offers from other universities, and had politely turned them all down. Chet Carrington's house, and Chris' vineyard were his home, and no offer could get him to leave.

At the end of September, Sondra Whitman arrived to meet with Dawn and Chris about the next year's workshop. After dinner at Hickory Park, the three began a discussion. They agreed that two instructors would be invited next year and one would concentrate on poetry, and the other on fiction. Invitations would be sent to high school poetry teachers, and the other class would be made up of fiction authors who had one book published. Sondra had offered that the Written Word would cover the added expenses. Dawn declined, politely, saying, "Chet left enough resources to fund all of this."

The conversation changed to Chris, and what his future plans were. As he began, Sondra interrupted, saying, "I have some good news for you. I met with the provost this morning, and your grant has received eight more years of funding, which will give you tenure.

Chris, do you remember what your original offer said?" He replied, as if he had read it yesterday, "To guide the next generation of poets to advance the quality of the written word in poetry, which will enhance the quality of life for humanity."

With a big smile, Sondra said, "I can't keep it a secret any longer. The Written Word is the company that supplies your grant. After your father died, sales of his books soared, and after expenses and a fair profit, there were excess funds available. I thought it would be a kind thing to do to advance your father's work, and do it through you. I hope you will accept." Both Dawn and he were shocked at the news, but they both thanked her, graciously, for the kindness. And Chris replied, in a shaky voice, "It would be an honor to accept the grant to further my father's legacy."

Chris thought, "The die has been cast. This is my home, and this is part of my career. Thank you, Dad."

Chapter 34

The next five years moved too quickly for Dawn and all who surrounded her. The accomplishments created by all were on the verge of astonishing!

Dawn was still shaping young people's minds with her literary workshops. Since the inception of the plan, first suggested to her by Chet in his will, thirty young scholars had developed their talents. Some were obvious, others had deep buried roadblocks that, at the start, kept them from reaching their full potential. Dawn had the God given gift of an educator, and any circumstance that kept her students from achieving were always overcome.

The original book, written by the Russell girls, had become a series. Each year's new class had added their imagination, and Dawn had given credit to Audry, who long ago had told her, "Give them their heads, let them run with it. Remember, destiny will guide them."

Sondra Whitman had been both patient, and generous. A portion of each book sold was given to the local chapter of the Women's and Children's Shelter, and the trickle down effect would last for generations. Dawn had such a deep feeling of satisfaction that Chet's goal, to touch one life, had been achieved.

The Chet Carrington Memorial Writer's Workshop had achieved a reputation, after nine years, of being the premier event for new writers from across America to attend. Some of the early attendees had become best-selling authors, and the program had a five-year waiting list. Dawn and Chris had agreed to keep the event small, classes of 20 proved to be the right amount. The exclusivity had made it even more popular.

Brent's photography career had become well-respected over the years. When he first introduced his retrospect, using only black and white images, the word traveled through social media, and his work was in demand in all the top galleries.

In an interview he did for a new, 1950's retro style magazine, called Black and White, The Image, he stated, "In our society, today, where a majority of communication is done on some form of electronics, without the benefit of one-on-one personal contact, a void has become pronounced in the human soul."

"I believe the resurgence of black and white photography is filling that void. In gallery shows across our nation, attendance is at an all time high. People come to view the stark contrast of black and white. They feel the raw emotion that is emitted from the image. Then, something miraculous occurs. An actual, face-to-face conversation, between two or more people, offering opinions about the work, sharing their feelings on how they were moved, emotionally. They are not texting, they are talking!"

As soon as the article was released, Brent received an invitation to have a solo show at the Littman-White Gallery in Portland. After he accepted, Chris offered him the use of his townhouse while he was there. As a secret ploy, Chris and Dawn had hatched an idea to surprise Brent on opening night. Chris had reserved the Gulfstream to take him, the Russell women, and Dawn to Portland. He would stay with Katherine, and the others would be in his mother's suite at the Benson.

They arrived at the gala one-half hour after it opened, and Brent was thrilled to see all of them. He took Dawn in his arms, and whispered in her ear, "I love you more, each passing day!" Chris and Wren viewed the show, together, and they both noticed that the common response to the images was, "This reminds me of…"

Lark enjoyed the 50's style banquet spread, especially the chocolate malts made with vintage malt-makers. Meadow was enthralled with the images, which she had seen before. She commented to Brent, "To see them, all together, your life's work, must be gratifying!" He replied, "I think the next exhibit we should attend is the one featuring your work from Tuscany. You captured some of the best light and shadow I have ever seen. When I get back home, we should talk to Dawn about the possibilities." With cheeks blushing , she thanked him, and with a smile on her face, she continued absorbing the exhibit.

Katherine had made reservations at Morton's for a late night supper for all of them, and the conversations lasted past midnight.

They all boarded the jet at 9:00 the following morning, and Chris had grabbed a copy of the OREGONIAN DAILY to read on the flight. Once they reached altitude, he began reading, and told the group, "We all made the society page, I'll read it to you. "The movers and shakers of Portland's art scene turned out in force last night for the opening of photographer Brent Makenzie's retrospect, a stunning display of black and white images. Pictured below is Katherine Cody, the matriarch of the Portland art scene, her son, Chris, a famous poet and professor, and their guests."

Chris began to laugh as he handed the paper to the rest of them to view, After looking, Dawn turned to him, and said, "De ja vu!"

Wren quietly said to Chris, "I don't get it. What's the joke?"
He replied, "I will show you an old photograph someday that will explain the whole thing."

Dawn noticed the two of them, talking quietly, and thought, "My God, it took them so long to find each other. My prayers have been answered, again."

Chapter 35

If one would be asked to describe the coming together of Wren Russell and Chris Cody, the responses would surely vary.

Katherine Cody: After careful consideration and due diligence, weighing all the long-term benefits, along with the short term return on investment, the merger was cautiously approved."

Dawn Carrington: "There are times in life when we take a new first step that will change our life direction, and once started, there is no return to the past. But sometimes it feels like a 500 pound weight is holding you back from taking the first step. It takes a huge amount of courage and fortitude to believe we can take the first step and start the journey, one step at a time."

Brent Makenzie: "Destiny and time are fickle partners. There are moments in life where they just can't agree on the timing of an event. Destiny says, "Today is the first day of the rest of my life." Timing replies, "What is the rush? You just finished yesterday a few hours ago. Patience!" This debate can go on for years, until timing, with a big smile, says to Destiny, "I just visited with your cousin, Fate, and he convinced me to let you have your way." With a huge sigh of relief, Destiny proclaims, "Thank you!"

Meadow Russell: "It would be comparable to taking an image at night. Even with the shutter, or eye, wide open, the amount of time the lens must be open to gather the subject must be perfectly calculated. If the shutter closes, or blinks, too soon, then the subject is lost, forever, never to be seen in that exact form, again."

Lark Russell: "The pitcher goes through all her antics, making all her adjustments, just to throw four straight balls for an intentional walk. Boring! Give me a finely turned double play for the final out any day. That's action!!!"

Sadie Russell: "We should pay more attention to swans. They take their time, courting slowly, showing courtesy and respect. When they finally mate, it is for life. Lesson learned!"

For Wren, the day it happened was as clear as a new windowpane. She could see herself, standing in front of him as she explained, "I do not work without a sweatshirt if it is below 70 degrees. The Pioneer Seed thermometer hanging on the shed says it's 58, so if you want me to work, pony up a sweatshirt now!" He had given her an old PSU sweatshirt, and when she put it on, she drank in his scent. She knew, at that moment, that he would fall in love with her. She also knew it would take time, but she was in no hurry. With the love she felt for him, she knew that half the battle had already been won.

For Chris, the love he now felt for Wren had taken years to develop. As he looked back, he would smile, thinking, "My father was the type of man who fell in love quickly, a man who knew what he wanted, and gave all of himself to the cause. I definitely missed out on that set of genes!"

They had worked together, side by side, putting the first plants in the vineyard, nurturing them through that critical, early period. He had watched her mature, from a gangly teenager, to a stunning woman. And it still had not happened.

The summer before her junior year at ISU, they were watering the newest set of plants. An irrigation sprinkler had become clogged, and together, they were dismantling it for cleaning. Their hands, covered with soil, touched, and Chris felt a spark that was new to him. He pulled his hand back, and looked into her eyes. It was as if a theatre curtain, long closed, had finally begun to open. He was in the front row, and a graceful beauty was being unveiled. The footlights were perfect, illuminating her outside beauty, as a single spotlight shone in her eyes, turning them into priceless emeralds.

He had to take a deep breath. He had never had this feeling before. He looked down to avert her gaze, trying to make sense of it all. She gently placed her soiled covered hands on his cheeks, lifting his face to hers. In a quiet, almost whisper, she said," Finally. You see me. I have waited for this moment for years. This is what love feels like. I know, I loved you at first sight." They stood, surrounded by their future, and embraced.

The courtship began. Chris felt he needed to approach Sadie and ask her permission, out of respect, to date Wren. He made an appointment to visit her, and she met him on the front porch. She

invited him to sit in one of the over-sized wicker chairs, and gave him an iced tea. After a few moments of uncomfortable silence, she said, "I don't think you drove all the way here to talk about the weather, so get on with it, please." He laughed, nervously, and replied, "I appreciate straight talk. Sadie, I am in love with Wren, and I am asking your permission to date her." It was her turn to laugh. "You know I have always been a God-fearing, church going woman, so pardon me when I say it's about damn time you asked. Christ, everybody in the county could see you two were meant for each other, except you! I am so thankful you finally opened your eyes, and your heart, to see my precious granddaughter.
Thank you for asking, you have my blessing, and I trust you will be good and gentle with her." Sadie gave him a hug and said, "Now get, I've got sheets to hang on the line."

  The following evening, Chris and Wren stopped at Dawn's after working in the vineyard. When Dawn saw them, she asked, "Well?" Wren laughed, then replied, "Chris has made the wise decision to date me. We thought you should know."

  Tears began to flow down Dawn's face as she put her hands together, as if in prayer, and whispered, "Thank you!"

  Chris looked at both of them, a quizzical look on his face, and both Wren and Dawn said, in unison, "Woman's intuition!"

  Dawn invited them to sit on the deck that hung out over the edge of the lake. She went inside, then returned with three wine chalices and an opened bottle of Merlot that Chris had given her the year he first arrived as Chet Carrington's son.

  After filling the glasses, Dawn gave a toast, "To the happy couple. You are blessed to discover each other, I am elated, and Chris, I know your father is smiling down on us. Peace be with both of you!"

Chapter 36

The next person who needed to be informed about Chris' good fortune was his mother. The night after telling Dawn, he placed the phone call, and he had to admit to himself that he was nervous. He so wanted her to be happy for him and Wren, and if she wasn't, he thought, it would be her loss.

After their normal chit-chat, he said, "Mother, I have wonderful news. I have fallen in love with Wren, and we are courting!" There was a moment of silence, than Katherine said, "When we were all together at Brent's opening, I could sense there was a deeper connection between you two than there had been, before. I always thought that there would never be a woman good enough for my son, but Wren, in my mind, passes with flying colors. Her grandmother and Dawn have done an amazing job raising those three girls. They represent the old fashion standard of politeness, genuine caring for others, and the simple fact that they are content with who they are. They have never presented a false façade, they are honestly real. That, son, is a very rare quality in today's society, and you should feel blessed to have Wren's love. Cherish it, nurture it, and revel in life's possibilities. I can only hope that you seize the opportunity for a fulfilled life in balance, not one sided like mine has been. Please tell Wren how happy I am with my son's choice! We will talk later. Love you."

When Chris hung up the phone, a sense of relief washed his mind. Knowing his mother was behind him meant he could concentrate on Wren and their future, without fighting a battle on another front.

He and Wren began to spend even more time together, both at work, and after hours. One day, during lunch time, they came up with a plan to follow as the fall term began. She was going to stay in the Maple-Willow-Larch complex until graduation, and they agreed that they should not be seen together on campus in a romantic way. Wren had said, "It is very important to me to keep up my grades, to learn all I can, so I can help someone have a highly successful winery." Chris laughed, and replied, "I want you to know you will always have a place at my business!" They kissed, tenderly, and returned to work.

Chris was now teaching his third group of poetry students, and they were in their sophomore year. On more than one occasion, during open discussion secessions, his students had remarked that he had changed in subtle ways. One girl had said, "Professor Cody, you seem to be deeper, emotionally, than last year. You are stressing to us the need to put more feeling into our compositions, to make it a challenge to move anyone who reads our work. I find that refreshing." One of the most surprising comments came from a four-star recruit who was the starting defensive end on the football team. He had stood up in class and said, "On Saturdays, my job is to disrupt the flow of the opponents offense, and wreck mayhem on the quarterback. Here, in class, I am learning how to develop my emotions, my passions. You could say I am getting in touch with my feminine side, but don't tell Coach, he would have a stroke." The comment brought out a burst of laughter from the class, but when it subsided, Chris perceived that more than one of his male students was mulling the comment over in their minds.

The love that he felt for Wren had reached the inner depths of his heart and soul. He made the decision to ask her for her hand in marriage, and began to devise a plot that would result in a heart-thumping surprise. He talked to Sadie, who agreed to be a co-conspirator. She would ask her three granddaughters to come home for a Sunday, fried chicken dinner. While they were there, she would remove her jewelry box from the closet, and ask all the girls to try all her rings on, in the guise of saying, "I am not getting any younger, and when I pass, these rings will go to you three. I want to see which ones fit you the best, and then I will list them in my will with your names. That way, there will be no arguing." The girls all enjoyed the process because each ring had a family history, and it was important for them to know, so, someday, they could pass down the story.

One ring fit Wren, perfectly. It was Sadie's grandmother's ring, an elegant red ruby mounted in yellow gold. The next day, Sadie took it to the jeweler in town, and found it was a size 7. That was the information that Chris needed for his plan.

He had asked Dawn for the name of the jeweler who had custom made Chet's ring and cufflinks, and she had sent him to Brooke, of b. shannon designs, in Winterset, Iowa.

Together, Brooke and Chris had selected a 2.5 carat, d color, VVS 1 clarity, round diamond that would be set in platinum.

Chris returned in two weeks to retrieve the most important possession he had ever purchased, and he was thrilled with the results. The ring was stunning!

On his way out of town, a long ago memory came to his mind. When he was a freshman at his private school, his literary teacher had the class read a novel about a photographer, a housewife, and covered bridges in Winterset. He made a note to himself to find and purchase a copy to pass along to his current class of students.

On his drive back to Ames, he stopped in Valley Junction in Des Moines at the theatrical shop. He purchased a long, blonde woman's wig, and a full black beard for himself. The following Saturday, over lunch, he explained his plan to Wren. "Next week is Homecoming and I want us to share a tradition. On Saturday, at midnight, I would love to meet you at the Campanile. If we kiss at midnight, then we will be true Iowa Staters." He pulled out the wig and beard, and said, "To add a little mystery, let's wear these, so no one will recognize us." Wren was laughing as she replied, "Who wears the wig, and who gets the beard?" He grabbed her and delivered a passionate kiss, adding, "That is just another reason I have given you my heart, I love your humor. Now, are you in?" With a warm smile, she replied, "OK, next Saturday night, at the Campanile, look for a guy in a beard, and kiss him at midnight. Can do!"

Chris spent the rest of the week visualizing the moment that was ahead of him. He had even walked to the grove, at home, sat in his father's chair, and explained his plan. He knew, in his heart, that Chet loved the idea.

That Saturday night was lit by a full moon that rose above the Campanile and the Memorial Union. Chris arrived at ten till midnight, dressed in jeans and a ISU hooded sweatshirt that framed his beard. He watched as Wren walked in from the east, her blond wig reflecting the moonlight. They embraced, and she said, "So, are you the one I am suppose to kiss at midnight?" He replied, "I think we should practice." He gently held her as they began a long, passionate kiss that lasted until the bells had finished their twelfth strike. They separated, and he whispered, "Now that we are official Iowa Staters, I would like to make one more thing official." He pulled his hood back, removed his beard, and got down on one knee. As he took her hand, and gazed into her eyes, he whispered, "I have been at this moment a thousand times in my mind. You are my last thought at night, my first at morning light. I wish, I hope, I pray, that I can live out my life beside you. Will you give me the honor of marrying you?" With that, he opened the jewelry box in his hand, then slipped the ring onto her finger. In the moonlight, the diamond shone as much as her eyes, covered with tears, as she held him close and whispered, "Yes!"

Chapter 37

The summer between Wren's junior and senior year ended up being full of possibilities. All three of the Russell girls would be spending time in Europe.

The American Association of Women's Softball had assembled an all-star team consisting of collegiate players who would travel through England, France, Spain, and Germany, playing those countries best in a tournament. Lark was the only player selected from the state of Iowa to participate.

Through a program at ISU, Meadow would be spending her time in Tuscany, photographing the entire region, and collecting local stories that would put a spotlight on their way of life. The program included the placement of a student in England, Scotland, Finland, and Spain, with the same assignment. The student who brought back the best work would be awarded a grant to publish a coffee table work, showcasing their work.

Wren would also be in Tuscany, visiting four different wineries. This opportunity was a trial experiment, funded by the viticulture course at ISU. A total of 12 students would participate, and in the end, all the information gathered would help American growers.

Before they all headed to Europe, Chris and Wren had written down their schedules, and figured out the time differences. This allowed them to visit by phone, once a week, and even though they knew the separation would be hard, Wren felt it was an opportunity she couldn't pass up, and Chris fully supported her decision. That was just part of being in love, and letting each other grow.

Chris knew he would be up to his chin in work that summer. He was working with a contractor on completing the wineries new facility. It would include state-of-the-art machines that would take the grapes from the crush to the fermentation process, a bottling room, and a small retail and tasting suite. The previous year's harvests had been sold to other local growers, and Chris was anxious to put the current year's bounty in his own barrels, to begin his and Wren's legacy.

Even though he worked from sun-up to past sun-down that summer, ending each day in total exhaustion, he always had trouble falling asleep. He still marveled about the speed and depth that his love for her had deepened. He compared it to a person never eating ice cream, and then one day, a door opened, and he was invited in to taste a double scoop of vanilla ice cream, stacked on a sugar cone. The experience was so totally overwhelming that, when offered another flavor, he declined, knowing it could not be better than what he had.

He missed her smile, her laugh, the sweetness of her lips, the gentleness of her touch. After they had become serious, she had explained that she wanted to save herself for the marriage bed, and it was an agreement that had almost been broken between them on more than one occasion. Chris knew that a moment of bliss and splendor was not as important as her beliefs. She had said, "Honey, when I walk down that isle to join you in holy matrimony, my white gown will truly mean purity." But oh, he could imagine!

When the three girls returned from their trip, Dawn had said, "It is a three ring circus, and I am the ringmaster!" Lark's team had lost in the championship game to the team from Germany, 2 to 1, but she said, "The best thing I learned is it takes mental toughness to compete in that many games in a row, and it doesn't matter what uniform you wear, we are all humans, all equals."

Meadow had returned with five-hundred images, and a three inch-binder full of stories from the people who made their living off the land. Brent offered to help her organize her photos, and said, "You are a good photographer, bordering on being a great photographer. I suggest you go through all of your images, and ask one question. "Would I go to the expense of having this enlarged to a 30x40, matte and frame it, sign my name on it, and show it in a gallery? If the answer is no, then discard it." She spent the next two weeks doing the culling process, and came back to Brent, showing him a portfolio that contained fifty stunning images. She sat at Dawn's dinner table, silently, as he looked at each one. By the time he had finished, his eyes were wet with tears. He said, in a shaking voice, " You have reached the level and insight in photography that I have yet to achieve. Before you is your first solo show, and I will help you make it happen. Congratulations!"

Wren came home looking even more mature, more assured, and even more beautiful. Working in the sun all day had given her skin the luster of gold, and her red hair was streaked, naturally, into countless hues and variations of red. When she hugged Chris on her return, he felt a loss of breath. He could not imagine living without her for the rest of his life.

She was very impressed with the new winery, and the knowledge she had gleaned in Tuscany would surely make their vintage a success.

One of the assignments they had given each other before she left was to write down the type of wedding each of them envisioned. One week before her senior term was to start, they met at Chris' house to barbecue steaks and compare lists. Each of them came with a mind-set of compromise. As they exchanged, and began reading, they both erupted in laughter. The lists were identical, down to the cake, decorations, where to have it, and who to invite. They both agreed that there would be only three hurdles to jump, Katherine, Dawn, and Sadie. But they were firm, knowing it would be their wedding, and it would go smoothly.

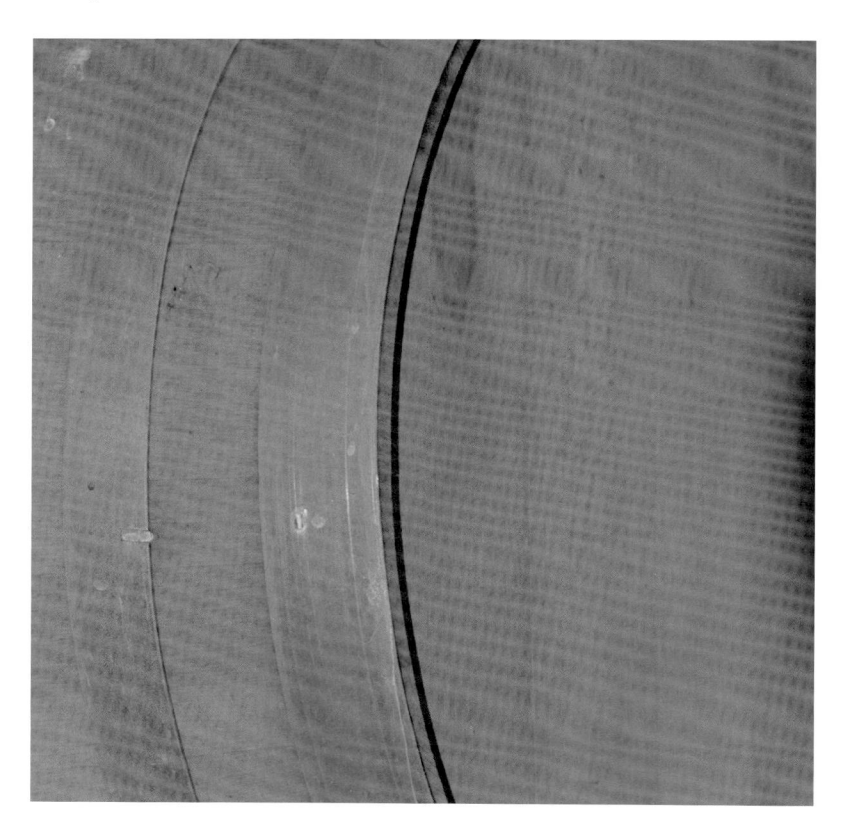

Chapter 38

The fall term began, and Chris welcomed his fourth group of freshman. Three of the new students had siblings who had gone through the earlier classes, and they had high expectations. The administration decided to move Chris to a larger facility, and they had decided on the Chester Carrington Memorial Hall, in the Morrill building.

To Chris, the move allowed him to see his father's portrait, three days a week, and he felt even closer to him in this space, where, years ago, he told a tragic love story. He thought, "Maybe, by the grace of God, a measure of passion, emotion, empathy, and imagination, still hangs in the air, patiently waiting, to help some student see, inside himself."

The fact that Chris was the son of Chet had never been public knowledge. He had explained to the Dean, when he accepted the position, that he preferred to make a mark on campus on his own, not in the shadow of his father. The college had always respected his wishes.

By the second week of the semester, the question finally came up, in class, "Professor Cody, you have a remarkable resemblance to the portrait of Mr. Carrington. Is there a story there?" Without pausing, Chris replied, " I can say, without a doubt, that I never met Mr. Carrington. I admire his body of work, and what he willingly gave to society. If my work as a writer and teacher could, someday, be mentioned, in the same breath as his, I would be blessed. I am sure you have all heard the urban legend, that all of us have a look-a-like, somewhere in the world. Evidently, he is mine." The subject never came up, again.

Along with his teaching duties, Chris had a crop of grapes to bring to harvest. Wren had suggested that he contact the horticulture professors on campus, and see if the students would like to experience a harvest. The professors liked the idea so much, they made it mandatory. Only students who had attained the legal drinking age could participate. Upon completion of the harvest, each one would receive a bottle of wine that Chris had purchased from a neighboring winery, since his vintage wouldn't be ready for years. Three bus-loads of students spent one day picking the grapes, and the harvest was complete.

With that task completed, he and Wren could focus in on their wedding plans. Sadie had insisted that Wren wear her mother's wedding dress. With tears of joy, she graciously accepted. It was a simple, pure white linen dress with hand crocheted flower petals on the hem. The dress was a perfect fit, no alterations were needed.

Chris would wear a gray, light-weight dinner jacket, black pants, black shoes, and a French cuff white shirt, complimented by a red tie and pocket square. He would wear his father's matched ring and cuff link set.

The best man would wear a blue, bankers striped suit, and the maid of honor would wear a short sleeved, blue silk gown that was floor length. The bridal bouquet would consist of three white Calla lilies, in honor of the Father, the Son, and the Holy Ghost.

Dawn had offered her home for the rehearsal dinner, and Katherine, as mother of the groom, made the arrangements to find a chef. After a thorough search, she had selected the chef who prepared all the important dinners held at the ISU President's house. Chris and Wren had given her only one stipulation, Iowa beef had to be the main course. The rest was up to her.

Dawn had also found a harpist and a cellist to perform at the reception, and she and Katherine were being very secretive about a wedding gift for the couple.

Chris and Wren had decided that on the invitations, three local charities would be listed if an attendee felt they needed to buy a gift. They had all the home provisions they needed, and felt it was important to help someone else out.

Sadie took the responsibility of the wedding cake. She explained to Wren that there were master cake bakers at church, one even baked full-time. Again, the couple gave Sadie one stipulation. No almond flavored anything, no cake, no mints, not anything! All other flavors were acceptable.

For the minister, they chose the new one at the Lutheran church in Story City. Her name was Evona Swenson. She had just accepted the call to be the senior pastor, and had spent the previous five years in a mega church on the south side of Minneapolis. Wren had been a life-long member in Story City, and Chris had started to attend, with her, on a regular bases.

      They both enjoyed the traditional service, and Pastor Swenson's no-nonsense style. The last major decision was the selection of a photographer. Chris had asked Brent, who declined, saying, "This is the most important day in your life, and I am looking forward to being with Dawn as we share the experience with you two. And I would hate it if I did the photos, and they didn't turn out. I would also caution you from asking Meadow, for all the same reasons. I do have a friend who is world class, I'll see what I can do."

      A week later, Brent called Chris to inform him that award winning photographer Cortney Kintzer would video the wedding and reception, and take candid stills. Chris thanked him, and asked about the cost. Brent laughed, saying, "It's already paid, my gift to you and Wren."

      They agreed that everything was under control, wedding wise, and now they could take more time just enjoying each other, and Wren could concentrate on her upcoming graduation from ISU.

Chapter 39

Chris was surrounded by his new, blended family, as Wren walked across the stage to accept her diploma, with honors. His mother had even flown in for the graduation, which deeply pleased him. Lately, she had shown signs that she was becoming a calmer, gentler soul.

They all went to Sadie's house for a steak fry, and Katherine had supplied all the wine from the Portland winery.

Meadow was getting ready for her first solo show, and Dawn and Brent were her sponsors. It would be held the first Saturday in August at the Norseman Gallery, the place where Chet had proposed to Dawn, decades ago, and where she had seen Brent, again, after twenty years.

The circles of life!

Lark had a full schedule of softball tournaments, from Miami to San Francisco, and all points in between.

Chris and Wren were in the middle of updating Chet's house, which is what everybody called it by now. Both bathrooms were being remodeled, the kitchen cupboards were refinished, and new carpet had been installed. All the interior walls had been painted, and the exterior looked beautiful with it's new covering of barn red paint with white trim.

They had debated about paving the driveway, but they both enjoyed the sound that car tires made as they crunched on the gravel.

The office would remain exactly as it had always been, and together, they refurbished the Adirondack chairs that sat in the grove, hoping they would last another twenty years.

The physical temptation between them had reached a fever pitch, so Wren was spending her nights in Dawn's spare bedroom. For Chris, knowing that the woman he loved was just a short distance away, connected by a blue slate path, provided many restless nights.

They continued to work, side by side, in the fields. Dawn would catch site of them as she relaxed on her deck, and later, she would say to Brent, "To love someone with all your heart is one thing, but to add in the opportunity to work and support each other on top of that is a true blessing." She laughed, and continued, " And, they are passionate. There have been times I have seen them working, and they just stop and gaze at each other. That led to kissing, and I thought I would have to turn the hose on them! I am glad they are waiting, and I am also glad we didn't!"

The summer raced by, and suddenly, there were two days left before the wedding. All the lists had been checked, and then the checks had been checked! Everything was perfect, and the weather forecast said clear skies, and 71 degrees. When Chris heard the temperature, he turned to Wren and said, "Honey, did you hear that? 71 degrees. No sweatshirt for you!" She grabbed him, held him close, and whispered, "I will be counting on you to keep my body warm."

Katherine had flown in early, and on the night before the rehearsal dinner, Chris and Wren were invited to Dawn's to dine with her and Katherine. Dawn had cooked chicken breasts on the grill, and a just picked salad from her garden was the perfect compliment to a dry red wine that Katherine had brought from Portland.

For dessert, they ate a delicious, luxurious cake that Dawn had been introduced to decades before. After Katherine took her first bite, she closed her eyes, and uttered, " This is delectable, what is it called?" Dawn answered, nonchalantly, "Better-than-sex cake." With a laugh, Katherine replied, "I wouldn't know, it's been so long!"

With that comment, Chris' face turned red from embarrassment, and Wren added, "I can honestly say I have no way to compare at the present time, but ask me in three days!" Chris raised both his hands, and said, " Please, enough of this topic!"

When the table was cleared, Dawn served coffee, and she said, "Okay you two, Katherine and I have something to talk to about." She motioned to Katherine, who produced a portfolio from her brief case. She slid it across the table to Chris and Wren, and they began to read it:

Northwoods Preservation L.L.C. conveys all it's rights and property to Christopher Cody, and his spouse, Wren Cody. The two properties, on Black Duck Lake, have an appraised value of $400,000 each, and bookend property owned by Dawn Carrington.

Todd Rosein-President-NP, L.L.C.
Katherine Cody-Chairwoman-NP, L.L.C.

Chris was speechless, and Wren was confused. She had yet to see the Carrington cabin, this was all new to her. He finally spoke, "Mother, what a wonderful gift, and I hope you know how much we appreciate it. And Dawn, it must feel good to you, knowing that some development company won't be coming in to ruin the solitude, the ambiance, that is found there."

She replied, "Well, it doesn't really concern me now, since I no longer own the property." She slid a piece of paper across the table to Chris, and said, "But you do!"

In front of him lay a quick claim deed, showing the transfer of the cabin property to him. Tears filled his eyes as she explained, "I know your father would want you to carry on his legacy, and that cabin and *Author*, were an important part of his life. I hope you and Wren find happy moments there, and both Katherine and I can only hope that, someday, you two will pass it on to your heirs. This is our wedding gift to you."

They all stood, and exchanged hugs. For Chris, it wasn't the dollar value of the transaction that was important, it was the long range possibility of his children walking in their Grandfather's shadow, feeling his presence, understanding the person that he was.

After they left, Chris and Wren walked to the pine grove, and sat in the chairs. Chris took her hand in his and said, "Years ago, the man, who I thought, had purchased those properties, had told Harry, the caretaker, his vision for the future. He said, "One day, a young couple in love will stop here, and simply enjoy the scent of the pines, soak in the music of the wind, gently caressing the boughs, creating symphonies that will never be replayed, always original. And with God's grace, and a little luck, they will experience the Northern Lights, painting the sky on a cold winter night, as they lay wrapped together in a sleeping bag, shivering from the sound of a lone wolf, calling it's mate."

Later, I had a vision of being in that sleeping bag with a redhead. Fate brought us together, and destiny will take us to that night. Would it be all right with you if we went to the cabin after our wedding?"

She rose from her chair, and tenderly sat on his lap. After she kissed him, gently, she whispered, "I will go anywhere with you. Any place we are together is home. And our home will be filled with love." They kissed deeply, and then realized that it was time to walk back to Dawn's, before the next natural step could happen.

As he left her at Dawn's door, she smiled and said, "Dream of me, tonight!"

And he did.

Chapter 40

The wedding rehearsal was performed in one take. All in attendance, including Pastor Swenson, wore ISU Polo shirts. The theme carried on from the succulent, prime rib dinner, to dessert. The chef had made individual cherry pies, a tradition that started on campus in 1920, and was a feature at VEISHEA each year.

All of the guests enjoyed the whipped cream topped delicacy as Dawn played standards from the American song book, ending the evening with her original song, Saving Grace, gently coaxing the Steinway to release it's golden, melodious tone.

A true sense of calm had fell on everyone, and, one by one, they quietly strolled through the vineyard, admiring the full, ripe fruit, inhaling the sweet scents, and enjoying a beautiful sunset.

The guests began to leave, knowing that tomorrow would be a day to remember. The weather forecast was perfect, and a new life would begin.

Chris and Wren came back to Dawn's to thank her and Katherine for such a fine evening, and Chris started to walk to his home. Wren slipped her arm through his, and whispered, "This time, tomorrow, I will be giving myself to you for the first time, and it will become the first night of the rest of our lives, together. I love you! Sleep well!"

As he continued to walk the blue slate path to his door, he felt blessed for all the family that had supported he and Wren today, and couldn't wait to say, "I'm married!"

Chapter 41

It was a picture perfect afternoon, fluffy clouds suspended in a robin's egg blue sky. A gentle breeze floated through the pergola, mixing the fragrance of heavily laden grape vines with the scents of pink, white, and red climbing roses that were in full bloom. The hour-glass shaped area that led to the alter was covered in blue grass, perfectly manicured, with chairs that were covered in white linen. All the guests had taken their seats, and were enjoying the heavenly, melodic strains of the harpist.

Pastor Evona Swenson stood under the rose covered rafters, with Sadie Russell's Bible in her hands, quietly going over the ceremony, one last time, with the groom and the best man.
As if on cue, the cellist began, and the maid of honor slowly walked towards the alter, taking her place opposite the best man. The music changed, and Wren began the walk towards her new life, her eyes locked in on his, a smile on her face. Tears slowly developed in his eyes as he watched her walk towards him, knowing his life, from this moment on, would be fulfilled.

Wren paused before ascending to meet Chris, and Pastor Swenson began, "We are gathered here today to witness the holy union of Wren and Chris. Who gives this woman into marriage?" Sadie, Meadow, and Lark stood, and Sadie announced, loud and clear, "Her sisters and I!"

Wren took two more steps, her hand touched Chris', and the Pastor said, " These two have written their vows. Wren, you may begin." She turned towards him, memorizing the face she would see each morning for the rest of her life, and began:

"My darling, this is the moment I have waited for my entire life. I believe every little girl dreams of finding her prince, and with God's blessing, I have found you.

My love for you started as a curiosity, a wonderment, and then it slowly evolved. I hid it from you, wanting to make sure it was from my heart and soul, not just a fantasy. When I knew you felt it, too, our love grew together, building layer on layer of trust, respect, kindness, and the art of becoming one.

We took our time, with you always saying, " You must be happy and content with yourself before we head towards a night of continuous tomorrows."

I love your patience. You let me grow as a person, unencumbered by a set of society's guidelines. I found myself, and today, I give all of my soul, love, and body to you, in trust that you will dedicate the same to me.

With this ring, I thee wed."

She slid a silver band on his finger, and he began his vows to her.

"To my dearest Wren, I stand before you on this day with all my faults and weaknesses. I trust that you will accept who I am, and offer me understanding, respect, and tenderness.

I stand before you on this day with a pure heart, free of thoughts of past loves, knowing you will be given all my love, unconditionally.

I stand before you on this day pledging I will listen, not only with my ears, but also my heart. I will consider your point of view, and support any endeavor you feel you need, to grow as a person. I will cherish the first sight of you each morning, and will offer a prayer of thanks each night for the love you have given me. I look forward to growing old with you, and looking back, together, at our wonderful life, and the legacy that we will leave behind.

I stand before you on this day, offering my mind, body, and soul, until I take my last breath. With this ring, I thee wed."

He gently slid a platinum band on her finger, and they kissed, tenderly. Pastor Swenson declared, "By the powers vested in me by the State of Iowa, I now pronounce you husband and wife." As the couple turned to face the guests, she continued, "It is my pleasure to introduce to you, Mr. and Mrs. Chris Cody!"

The guests stood as they applauded, many wiping tears from their eyes. The new couple slowly moved toward the reception, accepting congratulations along the way.

The maid of honor and the best man were still standing in the pergola with the pastor, admiring the newly married couple. She said, "Those two are surely blessed by God. Now, are you two ready?" They both nodded, yes, and Pastor Evona Swenson began, "Do you…"

An excerpt from *Full Circle*, The Carrington's story continues.
Publishing in Fall of 2015

Chapter 1

The early, hard frost had accomplished nature's mission. The leaves on the twenty hard maple trees that surrounded the green space at the winery were proud to show their brilliant hues of red. Chris and Wren Cody had planted the grove as a wedding present to themselves ten years ago. When he approached her with the idea he explained, "My darling, I want nature to duplicate your shear beauty. The deep, lush Bermuda grass will offer a stunning contrast to the vibrant reds of the maple trees in the fall, which will always remind me of your emerald eyes and luxurious mane of red hair." She blushingly agreed to the idea, and they had lovingly cared for the trees as if they were their children.

And it was children that had been the main attraction today. Twenty to be exact. All age five with a level of energy that, if harnessed, would surely run OPEC out of business. There were pony rides, a bounce house, snow cones, and a clown that could turn a handful of balloons into any animal a child could imagine. The birthday cake was shaped like the Campanile at ISU, it's layers rich in red and yellow, with buttercream frosting generously applied between. The children were instructed by Wren that it would be served, layer by layer, starting at the top, but she could tell, by the look in some of those mischievous eyes, that they would prefer to have the bottom piece, first!

Every birthday party needs a guest of honor, the person who could say that this was their special day. And today, that person was Chester Carrington Cody, nicknamed Cary, five-year-old son of Chris and Wren Cody, and grandson of the late Chet Carrington, famous author, and Katherine Cody, business magnet of the Pacific Norwest.